A HOUSE FAR FROM HOME

BUDGE WILSON

Cover by Ric Riordon

Scholastic Canada Ltd.

Canadian Cataloguing in Publication Data

Wilson, Budge.
  A house far from home

ISBN 0-590-71679-4

I. Title.

PS8595.I47H68 1986   jC813'.54   C86-094300-3
PZ7.W54Ho 1986

3rd printing 1990   **Printed in Canada**

Manufactured by Webcom Limited

To Glynis
my daughter, my friend

Contents

1. Bad news.. 1
2. Leave-taking 12
3. Jonathan Jackson 21
4. Aunt Marian.. 33
5. First day at school 41
6. Mildred 50
7. Letters... 60
8. Coach Zomer's decision 68
9. Lorinda gets mad.. 74
10. A trip to Toronto.. 83
11. Lorinda's birthday 89
12. The thief 101
13. The big game.. 109
14. A family of five 119
15. Home again 128

1
Bad news

January the first! Lorinda jumped out of bed, cold feet and all, and rushed over to the window. She always felt that if the new year's first morning was beautiful, the whole year would be special. If it was dark and stormy or even just drizzly and grey she would start having gloomy thoughts. What if Jessie runs away and we can't find her? What if Daddy's cough gets worse and worse? What if the Himmelmans and MacDermids move away from Blue Harbour? What if we get that crabby Miss Bennett for a teacher next September? What if James suddenly turns into a nervous wreck?

Jessie was Lorinda's two-and-a-half-year-old sister. Their father had chronic bronchitis and was often too sick to fish. The Himmelmans and Mac-Dermids were her friends. Miss Bennett taught grade 6 in the East Pines Consolidated School in the next county, but sometimes they switched the teachers around among schools. James was her seven-and-a-half-year-old brother, who was always (almost always) calm and collected. Lorinda (who was certainly not always calm and collected) wanted him to stay that way, just in case she fell apart in a million pieces some day.

It was 7:35. When Lorinda looked out the window, she could see the sun rising over Pony Island as red as an apple. Clouds close to the horizon had caught its light and turned a warm deep rose colour. The sea was calm like glass — like oil — and the snow from the previous night's fall was lying still and quiet on the land.

Lorinda sighed with relief. It would be a good year. She looked over at Jessie, still fast asleep by the window, and knew her little sister would be safe for another three hundred and sixty-five days. She could hear her father coughing downstairs, but still, he was definitely getting better. Miss Bennett probably preferred to do her crabbing at the East Pines Consolidated School, and Lorinda was so sure James would stay calm that she even felt a little nudge of annoyance. Sometimes it bugged her that he never flew off the handle and could always see both sides of any argument. She'd like it if just once he'd get so mad he'd slam the door right off its hinges.

Suddenly Lorinda realized how cold it was. Quickly she put on a pair of tights and her jeans, then her big wool Lopi sweater with the pattern on the shoulders, a Christmas present from Aunt Joan. You could be warm in that sweater at the North Pole.

She looked at herself in the mirror. What she saw was a tall, skinny girl of almost eleven. She looked at her long straight black hair and at a face that was neither pretty nor ugly, but somewhere in between. Once she had overheard her father saying to her mother, "Give her time, Lydia. Wait till she's fifteen or sixteen. She's got good bones. The Dauphinee women are always gawky till they get older, but when they start to bloom, watch out!" Lorinda wasn't exactly sure what all that was about, but she thought it was a sign of something good that lay ahead for her.

She took another quick look out the window at the sunrise, then went downstairs to the kitchen.

"Hi, Mummy!" she cried, giving her mother a big hug. "Happy New Year! I've got it all worked out. It's going to be the best year of our lives. Everything's going to be perfect!"

Lorinda felt her mother's arms tighten around her. Then the arms dropped and her mother went back to the double boiler on the stove. She stirred the porridge hard, not answering Lorinda's cheery greeting. Just then James came in, still in his pyjamas and without his glasses on. He was scratching his chest, rubbing one eye and yawning.

"James!" said Lorinda. "Did you see the day? Extra gorgeous. Peaceful and red, like a picture out of a book. And you know what that means — a perfect year from start to finish!"

James yawned again. "Good," he mumbled. "That's real good news. Hi, Mummy!"

"Hi, darling," said his mother, leaving her porridge long enough to give him a hug. "Happy New Year!"

James drew back and tried to focus on her face. "What's wrong?" he asked.

"What do you mean, what's wrong?" said Lorinda impatiently. "Mummy just gave you a big hug and wished you a Happy New Year. What are you looking for, fireworks?"

"I can feel something funny in her arms," said James, fishing for his glasses. "And her voice isn't right." He stared hard at his mother. "Something's wrong."

Lorinda crawled out of her own skin long enough to really look. He was right. There was something tight and closed-up about her mother's face. She looked, for Pete's sake, as though she might *cry*. Lorinda put her hands on her hips and faced her mother.

"What's the matter?" she demanded. "We're not babies, you know. Tell us! You can even" — Lorinda looked uneasy — "cry if you want to. Is Daddy okay?" Oh gosh, she thought, what ever happened to my beautiful day, my beautiful year?

Mrs. Dauphinee sat down and began twisting her apron into a ball. "Everything's fine," she said, smiling a sick, sad smile. "Everything's just wonderful. Like Lorinda said, it's a lovely morning."

But when all three of them turned to look out the window, they saw the calm sea ruffling up and clouds gathering overhead. A few scattered raindrops slid down the pane.

Lorinda smacked the side of her face with the palm of her hand. *"Red sky in the morning: sailors take warning,"* she chanted. "I'm usually smart about weather. How could I have been that stupid?"

Then she turned to her mother and said anxiously, "Mummy, listen. You might as well tell us what's wrong. I'd rather worry about something real than something I might imagine. *What's wrong?"*

Mrs. Dauphinee smoothed out her balled-up apron and held it in her hands. Then she buried her face in it and cried. James went over and patted her shoulder, but Lorinda didn't know what to do. She'd never seen her mother like this. It made her feel frozen solid inside and out. Mrs. Dauphinee was muttering something into her apron and hiccupping.

"Sorry. I'm so sorry. I should have told you

sooner but I wanted us to have a perfect New Year's Day first."

"Told us what?" demanded Lorinda and James in unison.

Mrs. Dauphinee sighed a long, quavery sigh, then blew her nose on a piece of paper towel she had grabbed off the counter. When she turned to face them, her nose was red and her eyes were wet, but she was smiling.

"There!" she said, her voice calm again. "I'm fine now. I guess there's no use pretending it's just any old New Year's Day with nothing but the roast sea duck and the mince pie to think about. Sit down, both of you."

Lorinda and James drew their chairs up close to the kitchen stove, though they both knew the cold they were feeling wasn't just a matter of temperature. Lorinda hugged herself and tried to stop her teeth from chattering. "Hurry," she said.

Their mother sat with her hands in her lap. She wasn't fidgeting any longer. "It's not good, what I have to say," she began. "But then again, it's not the end of the world either. We may even look back sometime and see it as a wonderful experience."

"Mummy!" exclaimed Lorinda. "You're not telling us a single thing!"

Mrs. Dauphinee looked up at them and laughed. "Neither I am," she admitted. "Okay, it's like this." She took a deep breath. "Your dad's cough isn't getting any better. In fact, the doctor says it's worse. So he says we have no choice. We have to move him out of this damp, raw climate and take him where it's warm and dry."

"Move!" Lorinda almost yelled the word.

James dug her in the ribs and whispered, "Shh!"

"Not forever," said Mrs. Dauphinee. "Just till it's summer again. And only this year. The doctor says if your father can get a base of really good health under him he'll be stronger all over. Then when there are flu bugs and things going around, he maybe won't catch them so fast." She didn't add that Dr. Semple had said that at the moment Mr. Dauphinee's health was in a "dangerous state." She didn't like to think about what *that* meant. She just knew that if going to a warm place was going to help him get better, that was what they were going to do.

"Well," said Lorinda slowly, suddenly starting to see good things about this unexpected news, "I suppose that isn't so terribly awful. Where are we going? Australia? Egypt? Disneyland?" The move was looking better and better every minute.

Her mother looked at her steadily for a moment or two. "That's the hard part, Lorinda. That's why I'm crying. You see, we can't *all* go."

Lorinda's mouth fell open. She hardly dared ask the next question. "Who's going where? And who isn't?"

Mrs. Dauphinee looked miserable. "Your father and I are going to Texas to stay with my brother, your Uncle John, the one you've never met. He's got a ranch and a lot of land. I write to him often, and when he heard how bad your father's cough was, he invited us to come down and soak up the sun till July. Then we can come back here and soak up our own sun."

Lorinda stared at her. "But why do *you* have to go? You're not sick. We all need you here, maybe even more than Daddy does." She felt mean saying this, but it came out without any warning.

Mrs. Dauphinee sighed again. "It's not that simple," she said. "Dr. Semple says there's a chest clinic forty-five kilometres from Uncle John's. If he's as sick as he is right now, your dad shouldn't be driving. He needs a taxi-driver — me. Besides, sometimes he'll have to stay overnight. There has to be someone to drive John's car back to the farm for him."

"Why not take our truck?" Lorinda clung to the hope that this awful thing might not have to happen.

"Oh, Lorinda," said her mother, "don't think we haven't thought of all those things." She began twisting her apron again. "Our truck is so old that it wouldn't survive the trip down there and back. I hate to be talking about money all the time, but you know yourself that we don't have enough for a new truck."

"And *us?*" Lorinda's throat felt tight and her voice sounded thin and scraped. "Why can't we go too?"

Mrs. Dauphinee's apron looked like a long, knobbly string. "Because John's house is hardly big enough for two people. Six would be impossible. Besides, the nearest school is eighty kilometres away. So . . ."

"So?"

"So your Uncle Harry in Peterborough — your dad's brother — has invited you to come and stay there with them. He and Aunt Marian have no children, and they've got two extra bedrooms." She sighed. "I'm told it's a pretty house and a nice city. Lakes and rivers nearby. Hills. And not far from Toronto."

"And school?" asked James, his voice hardly more than a whisper.

"You'll be able to go to school there. You'll meet a lot of new friends and see a lot of new places and have a lot of new adventures."

Later that afternoon, sitting on "Glynis's Thinking Rock" down at the beach, Lorinda tried to describe to herself exactly how she felt about her mother's news.

"I feel," she said aloud, staring toward the horizon while a heavy rain poured down her face, "as though my stomach has fallen right out of my body. I feel like I'm just one big empty aching space. I feel like it's going to rain on me for ever and ever."

But now, still in the kitchen, she said, "When are we going?"

"The day after tomorrow. Oh, I'm so sorry. I know I should have told you sooner, but I just couldn't bring myself to do it."

The day after tomorrow boomed inside Lorinda's head like a gong. It was so soon!

"What about Jessie?" she asked. Jessie, her Jessie, with all that black curly hair. The only curly hair in Blue Harbour.

"I'm sorry, Lorinda. She has to come with your father and me. She's just too young to send off alone for six months."

And so are we! So are we! Lorinda wanted to yell. But she just stood like a stone and said nothing. James hugged his mother and started to cry. Lorinda moved close and patted her hand. "Not your fault," she muttered, and then went out to the back porch.

She put on her boots, her ski jacket, her sou'-wester hat and her mitts, and strode off through the rain, all the way up to The Patch — the place where they picked blueberries in the summer. No one could hear her or see her there, so she sat down on a granite rock and howled like a coyote. She even beat her fist against the stone. She was angry, but she had no idea who she was angry at. She was sad beyond explaining. And she was afraid.

2
Leave-taking

The next day, their last in Blue Harbour, Lorinda didn't wake up until 8:30. It had taken her a long time to get to sleep the night before because her mind had been turning upside down and inside out. She crawled out of bed and walked slowly to the window. Jessie was sitting up in her cot dressing and undressing her favourite doll. On, off, on, off went the clothes.

"Hi," said Jessie.

"Hi, yourself," said Lorinda, who could hardly bear to look at her little sister. In six months, she thought, she'll even *look* different. She might even forget me. Lorinda closed her eyes against such a terrible thought. Then she pulled the curtains open and looked out.

The snow had melted in last night's rain, and the sun was shedding its light on a blue sea flecked white by a strong north wind. She could tell it was cold because the fishermen on the Government Wharf were slapping their hands together and stomping up and down. Weather in Nova Scotia changed very quickly. It was often warm one day and way below zero the next. Snow on Tuesday, rain on Wednesday. Even the weather people on the radio sometimes sounded confused.

That morning, lobster boats dotted the bay with bright dabs of green, orange and red. The men on the boats were removing the lobsters before letting the traps slip back into the water, their colourful buoys bobbing. The view from her window had never looked more beautiful. Lorinda sighed. She went over to the little cot and picked up a surprised Jessie and hugged her till she squealed.

"Hey!" gasped Jessie. "What you do?"

"I'm hugging you, stupid," said Lorinda. "That's what."

If only she could pack Jessie in her suitcase along with her baseball mitt and her new skates and the diary Aunt Joan had given her for Christmas. For that matter, if only they could go to Aunt Joan's instead of Aunt Marian's. But Aunt Joan had a houseful of kids already. Aunt Marian was so . . . she was so . . . Lorinda fished around in her head for the right word. So *tidy*. So stiff. So thin-lipped. She never had any mud on her shoes. It was impossible to imagine her kissing them goodnight or telling them stories. At ten-going-on-eleven, maybe you're supposed to be too old for all that stuff, Lorinda thought, but she knew that really wasn't true.

"Well!" she said right out loud, "I'd better stop thinking like *that* or I'm going to wreck my last day here. I'll just have to shove all those thoughts to the back of my brain, at least until tomorrow."

"Huh?" inquired Jessie, pausing in the act of taking Matilda's pants off. "What you say?"

"Nothing important," sighed Lorinda over her shoulder as she started downstairs for breakfast.

Mrs. Dauphinee was making pancakes — Lorinda's favourite. Mr. Dauphinee was sitting beside the stove in the old rocker. Both of them were smiling hard, and they both cried out, "Good morning, darling!" as though it were Christmas. But that didn't fool Lorinda. After all, she was acting the same way.

"Hi! Hi! Hi!" she greeted them, dancing a little jig across the floor to the country and western tune that was playing on the radio. It would be a relief to see James. Just as he didn't go in for wild rages or gloomy depressions, he wouldn't play this silly cheerfulness game either. Her mother was even *singing* as she flipped the pancakes over.

Lorinda was right. James came stumbling into the kitchen, shortsighted and sleepy, and gave his mother a long, slow hug. Then he went and put his arm around his father's shoulders for a moment.

14

When he sat down at the table, he said, "I'm hungry. Smells good."

Great, thought Lorinda. James knows what to do, as usual. He's put an end to all that stupid singing and dancing around. Now we can be natural with each other again.

And they were. They talked about Texas and Ontario, and when Mrs. Dauphinee brought Jessie down, they told her all about their plans. She shrieked and cried for about five awful minutes, then she settled down and got excited about Texas.

"Send us letters, eh, Jessie?" said James.

Lorinda stared at him. So did Jessie, who said, "Huh?"

"Send us lots of your pictures," went on James. "That'll make us feel near you."

Lorinda grinned. She loved Jessie's pictures, especially the ones of people — one circle, two eyes, a belly-button and four sticks.

"Will the schools in Ontario be really hard?" asked Lorinda, finally letting out one of the things that had kept her awake the night before.

"Not specially," answered her father. "They take thirteen years to get through school and we take only twelve. At the end we're in just about the same place. So it should be fine. It may not be a cinch, but it certainly won't be extra hard."

Lorinda felt as though she could breathe normally again. With that big worry out of the way, maybe she'd be able to survive after all.

Just as they were about to settle down to the dishes, Duncan and Fiona MacDermid, their red hair and freckles bright in the morning sun, arrived at the back door.

"We've come with going-away presents!" announced Fiona before Duncan had a chance to speak.

"Nice ones!" added Duncan, almost shouting. "Right out of our shop. Mom said they had to be extra terrific."

They were gift-wrapped and tied with fancy ribbons, the ones saved for weddings or for customers who were willing to pay extra for them.

Lorinda and James opened their gifts while Duncan and Fiona each had a pancake. James' present was a set of twelve little clay pots for starting seeds, each decorated with an intricate design. "Mum remembered that you like growing things," said Duncan. "She says she bets you'll end up being a farmer some day. She loves that cactus you gave her last month."

James smiled and smiled. He was already deciding what he'd put in each pot. What a great present!

Lorinda's gift was a calligraphy pen.

"We all know what a good artist you are," said

Duncan. "Now you can get to be the best letterer in Ontario." He pointed to the present. "There's a book inside the box that tells you how."

Fiona was thinking it was just as well she'd spoken up when they first arrived, because she hadn't had a chance to get a single word in since then. "We all thought," she blurted out before Duncan could start again, "that they were good presents for people who need to keep busy and forget how lonely they are."

The silence in the kitchen seemed to last half an hour. Finally Lorinda took a deep breath. "Let's go pick up George and Glynis," she said, "and go skating on Granite Pond. The ice should be really neat today. It may be our last chance. They tell me Ontario is covered up with snow all the time."

"Dope!" whispered Duncan to Fiona, as he shoved her out the door.

*   *   *

At the Himmelman house, George and Glynis were in the kitchen, wrapping up more gifts.

"Sorry," said George, sticking a final piece of scotch tape on one of the parcels. "We didn't have enough warning to get anything new. Even the MacDermid store was closed for the holidays."

"So," continued Glynis, who was James' special friend, even though she was almost two years younger than he was, "we're giving you stuff we found in our own house. Here." She handed her gift to James. "Open it!"

He did. Inside, in a little oval frame made of brass, was a picture of Glynis sitting on her Thinking Rock.

James smiled a sad, slow smile. "I like it a lot," he said.

Then Lorinda opened her present. It was a big hardcover book with lines in it.

"It was Dad's," said George. "He used it for his law stuff. But he says you'll be able to put things in it that are more interesting. You can use it for practising your calligraphy."

Then they all laughed, because it was obvious now that everyone had known about this trip before Lorinda and James.

"Now I understand why you were in such a bad mood last week," said Lorinda to Duncan.

"You got it!"

They all went out to Granite Pond and skated for almost two hours. The ice was like a giant mirror after the rain. Lorinda and James even forgot for a while that it was the second worst day of their lives.

Tomorrow, they expected, would be the very worst. They would leave, which was terrible. They would arrive, which would probably be worse. And

18

in between was the airplane. Neither Lorinda nor James said a word about this, but the thought of the plane was scaring them half to death. They might not even have to worry about arriving at Aunt Marian's, since the plane was sure to crash somewhere in the dark forests between Halifax and Toronto.

*   *   *

That night, Lorinda and James pressed their ears to the heat registers in the upper hall and listened to their parents talking.

"Oh, Jim," they heard their mother say, "I hope they'll be all right. It's so long. Six months!"

"They'll be fine," said their father. "Just look at Lorinda. That girl is made of tough stuff. She goes through life with both fists up. No one's going to walk over *her*."

"Well," sighed Mrs. Dauphinee. "You're probably right. But I worry about James. He's such a gentle kind of person. He doesn't go charging through life like a moose the way Lorinda does. He's so *quiet*. Will people understand that? They might even think he's dumb. And some people expect boys to be sort of, well, *belligerent*."

The kids heard Mr. Dauphinee chuckle. "Listen, Lydia," he said, so softly that they could hardly hear, "if there were odds on this thing, I'd lay my money on James. He may not make a lot of noise, but he's got a different kind of strength. It's like he's about ninety years old under his skin."

Mrs. Dauphinee gave a little laugh. Their father continued. "He thinks. He looks around. He understands people, even the nasty ones. If someone is mean to him, he'll just sit down and try to figure out why. His sense of justice — that's what'll carry him through."

There was a silence. Lorinda and James strained to hear more.

"Don't you worry for one second," their father said. "They'll be one hundred percent, four-star okay." And that's all they could make out.

Downstairs, Mrs. Dauphinee turned over and buried her face in the pillow. "I hope you're right," she whispered.

Lorinda and James stood up. "Well," declared Lorinda, grinning, "I guess we'll be one hundred percent, four-star okay!"

James went into his room and closed the door. He stood for a moment with his back to it. "I hope you're right," he whispered.

3
Jonathan Jackson

The next morning there was so much to do that they almost forgot to say goodbye to Petunia. Petunia was their cow. Mr. Hyson was going to look after her till they returned.

But they did remember, just in time. They went out to the barn, where Lorinda laid her cheek on old Petunia's face. James hugged the cow's large, warm, soft neck, but he couldn't say goodbye. There seemed to be a rock in his throat.

On the trip to the airport, everyone was very quiet. It's going to take all my energy, thought Lorinda, just to keep from crying. If that means not talking all the way to the airport, then it's going to be a silent trip.

Mr. and Mrs. Dauphinee made a few attempts at cheerful conversation, but no one responded. Only Jessie, sitting on Lorinda's lap, kept up a string of talk. "Look! Big dog! . . . Me thirsty . . . Why nobody talk? . . . Wanna go pee . . . Let's have a picnic . . . Lorinda hold me too tight."

Finally, Mr. Dauphinee turned on the car radio and they did their thinking to a background of old-time fiddle music. James sat with his hands in his lap, looking out the window.

At the airport, everything happened almost too quickly. They parked, unloaded the six suitcases, found the Air. Canada wicket, and checked their baggage. Mr. Dauphinee asked for window seats near the washroom, and Lorinda and James were given the boarding passes which would let them on the plane. Then suddenly it was time to go. Lorinda had her speeches all ready. They were short, and she managed to say them without sounding like she wanted to cry.

To her father she said, "Bye, Daddy. Hurry and get well." To her mother she said, "Bye, Mummy. Have lots of sun baths. Write us every week." To Jessie she just said, "Bye, Jessie. Don't forget us." Then she turned right around and marched through the exit to the plane.

James didn't say a word. He hugged his mother, his father and Jessie and looked at them all for a moment, as though he had a lot of things he wanted to say. Instead, he waved his hand very slowly, then wheeled around and raced after Lorinda.

Mr. Dauphinee picked up Jessie and started off toward the car. "See?" he said. "They're both going to be perfectly all right." If he had looked at his wife at that moment, he wouldn't have been too sure if *she* was going to be perfectly all right. But they were in a big crowd and it was all he could do to see where he was going. By the time he did look at her, she had rearranged her face and looked just fine.

*   *   *

From the moment they stepped on the plane, Lorinda and James had no time to think about homesickness. "We were just too busy hoping we'd stay *alive*," Lorinda was to say later.

They couldn't believe the airplane. From the inside it looked gigantic, like a long sausage-shaped theatre.

"How on earth can this thing stay up in the air?" Lorinda asked the stewardess who showed them their seats.

"Well," she answered, smiling, "it's a pretty hard thing to explain in just five minutes. But believe me, it will. I've been on one hundred and twelve flights, and on every one of them the plane stayed up."

That made Lorinda feel a little better — until she realized this was the stewardess's one hundred and *thirteenth* flight. She wanted to ask her if she was superstitious, but the stewardess was still talking.

"My name's Jean," she was saying. "If you want

me for anything, push that little button on your armrest. Here are some books to read" — she handed them two copies of *OWL* — "and some gum to chew. Chew it hard when we take off and land, to make your ears feel good. Bye now." She gave them each a little pillow before leaving.

A tall, handsome man entered the plane, checked the seat number and sat down beside Lorinda. He was older than her father, and he looked strong enough to protect them from almost anything. He'd be able to look after their fears, she thought, starting to relax. But then she noticed he was staring straight ahead, his face as white as paper.

Lorinda wasn't one bit shy. She watched him for a moment and then said, "You look awful. Are you okay? Can I get anything for you? Like a blanket or something?"

When the man looked at her, Lorinda could see he was embarrassed as well as miserable. "It's nothing . . ." he said.

"I'm Lorinda," she said, "and this is James."

"It's nothing, Lorinda," he repeated. Then he pressed his lips together so hard they disappeared.

"Are you *sure?*"

Now the man was sitting back in his seat with his eyes closed. He opened them for a second. "It's really nothing," he said. Lorinda thought he looked a bit like a lizard blinking in the sun.

"Well, I hope you're okay, because it's almost time for take-off."

At that, the man moaned out loud and then blushed. "I guess there's no point trying to hide it," he said miserably. "I'm scared to death of flying."

Lorinda sat up very straight. "You have nothing to worry about, Mr. . . ."

"Jackson. Jonathan Jackson. Jon is fine."

"Okay, Jon. We're safe as churches. Look at that wing. I'm sure it knows what it's doing and it sure is big. Lookit, I'm gonna switch seats with James. He's so calm, people feel better just being around him."

James, of course, had overheard everything. He began to feel the way he always did when Jessie was frightened. Even if he was scared blue of the same thing, he acted very brave so she'd feel safe. And half the time this took away some of his own fear too.

"Hi, Jon," he said as he crawled over. "How come you never flew before? We're only seven-and-a-half and ten-and-three-quarters, and look at us."

Mr. Jackson laughed weakly. "I *have* flown before, but it's always the same. Mostly I try to arrange my business and my life so I can use trains. But this time I had no choice. It's an emergency board meeting, and I have to be in Toronto by four o'clock this afternoon. Usually all our meetings are in Halifax, but not this time."

"Why?"

"Well, I'm not sure you'd understand."

Lorinda frowned. Adults were always saying things like that. "We might," she said. "You never know."

Mr. Jackson grinned, pale but friendly. "Our company may merge — join up — with a Toronto firm. We have to decide by tomorrow morning if we want to do it."

"Couldn't you have switched places with someone else?" asked James.

"No," said Mr. Jackson. "It's an important meeting. Besides" — he paused and his pale face turned red — "I'm the Chairman of the Board."

James just looked at him for a moment. "I won't tell a soul," he said. Then he fished in his pants pocket and found a grungy-looking bent stick of gum. "Here. If you chew this, your ears won't pop."

When the engines started, thrumming so hard it felt like the plane would fall apart, James was so worried about Mr. Jackson that he almost forgot to chew his own gum. What if he was sick all over his briefcase? What if he fainted dead away? He looked like he wasn't even breathing. He certainly wasn't chewing.

"Chew!" whispered James.

Mr. Jackson chewed.

Then, in the most amazing way, they felt the plane lift off the ground. Lorinda pressed her nose to the window. More quickly than she could believe possible, the trees became bushes, the cars turned into dinky toys and the buildings looked like Monopoly houses. "James!" she gasped. "It's so beautiful, I don't even care if the plane does crash. Jon, look! Look at all the tiny houses!"

But Mr. Jackson wasn't ready to look. "Later," he said, grabbing the chair arms so hard his knuckles turned white. "Maybe later."

But James was looking. The wonder of it was filling his eyes and all he could say was, "Oh, Lorinda!"

Lorinda gazed around the inside of the plane. "What on earth are all those people reading newspapers for?" she asked in amazement. "They're missing all this wonderful stuff. They can read their newspapers at home, for Pete's sake." Then she turned to James. "You get to have the window seat on the way home."

Now they were very far up, and James started to feel like an astronaut. He could imagine going higher and higher, until the earth became a globe beneath him. Far below he could see forest land, with lakes shining like little puddles here and there, and roads straggling through the green-black woods like skinny strings.

By the time the stewardess brought their dinner, they could hardly remember having been afraid. Mr. Jackson, however, only stared at his food and passed his hand over his eyes.

"Take whatever you want," he said to Lorinda and James. "I'll get something to eat when — and if — we get to Toronto."

"The pie for me," said Lorinda as she reached over for his plate.

"Me for the chicken," said James, helping himself.

Suddenly there was a *click-click-sputter*, and a voice came over the loudspeaker.

"Please fasten your seatbelts and refrain from smoking. We're going through a bit of turbulence and we'd like you to remain seated." The message was repeated in French.

"A bit of turbulence!" exclaimed Mr. Jackson as the plane lurched and dropped and rose again. "A *bit!* Oh — my — gosh!"

The stewardess was suddenly there, speaking to Lorinda and James. "This is nothing to worry about," she said. "It happens all the time. Just look on it as a kind of carnival ride. We should be out of it in fifteen minutes or so."

"If I live that long," muttered Mr. Jackson.

"We're okay," said James. "But Jon could use some help," he added, indicating Mr. Jackson.

"Oh, dear," she said, "I don't know how much I can do for him. It looks like airplane phobia to me. That's more than just fear. It's the same sort of terror that some people feel around snakes, or in closed elevators."

She leaned down. "Mr. Jackson," she said, "is there anything I can do to help you?"

"No," he said, keeping his eyes tightly shut. "Just let it be over. I'm going to spend the rest of my life on solid ground. It's not just the fear, it's the humiliation."

After the stewardess left, James looked at Mr. Jackson. "My dad says it's okay to be scared. He says men don't have to be giants all the time."

Again Mr. Jackson smiled. "Your dad sounds like a very smart man, James," he said.

Suddenly they were above the clouds and out of the turbulence. Below them, the clouds looked like a deep, soft mattress, thick enough to hold up a whole fleet of planes.

"Look, Jon!" yelled Lorinda. "Just look at that really great safety net!"

"Thanks, Lorinda," he said, "for trying."

It seemed hardly possible, but only a few minutes later the loudspeaker announced that they were approaching Toronto. Lorinda's stomach shot down into her snow boots. Now that it was obvious they were going to survive the journey, they had to worry about what was coming next. It was easy to act brave about planes when you were trying to help a man with airplane phobia, especially when the flight lasted less than two hours, but what was ahead of them was going to take six months to live through. James was sitting very still, with a line between his brows.

Mr. Jackson's eyes were closed and he was muttering, "The *landing*," over and over.

"Chew!" said James, and Mr. Jackson chewed.

Suddenly Lorinda felt like crying — and angry with Mr. Jackson, both at the same time. "The plane's going to land just fine, Jon Jackson," she snapped. "And even if it cracks up, we'll all be dead in two seconds and won't even know what hit us. In ten minutes, you're going to be off this airplane and on the way to your lovely meeting, whistling a tune and feeling just dandy. But we've got six whole awful months ahead of us! You haven't even *asked* anything about us!"

"Hey, Lorinda," said James, "I don't think he can help it."

Mr. Jackson's hands still grasped the arms of the chair so tightly that his fingers looked like wax. But he opened his eyes long enough to look at Lorinda and then at James.

"You're both right," he said through chattering teeth. "This isn't a fear you can cure by just *telling* yourself to be brave. Take my word for it. It's a fact. But" — and here he looked sadly at Lorinda — "I could perhaps *try* to think about someone else for a while. It might even help. Okay, then" — he smiled a weak, sick smile — "what's ahead for you in Toronto?"

Lorinda told him the whole story and Mr. Jackson really listened, even though his mind was still three-quarters on his own terror. By the time she was through, they were on the ground, taxiing over to the terminal.

"There!" she said. "See? We made it!"

Mr. Jackson suddenly looked a little more like a board chairman. Colour was beginning to come back into his face and he was smiling at them. He unbuckled his seatbelt as the plane came to a stop.

"Thanks, kids," he said warmly, mopping the sweat from his brow with a large handkerchief. "You really helped." He still looked embarrassed as he straightened his tie. "Would you write down your Peterborough address for me on this card? I might be up there on business sometime in the next six months. If things turn out as badly as you fear, maybe I could help *you* for a change."

Lorinda wrote quickly, then passed the card back.

"I hope it won't be as awful as you think," Mr. Jackson went on. "Peterborough's a good place and — well, maybe Aunt Marian will turn out to be a really nice lady after all. Life is full of surprises." He chuckled. "Look at me, for instance. Did I know when I woke up this morning that I was going to be rescued by a couple of kids? Now" — and he shook hands with them both — "good luck, you two. Try to be happy."

They said goodbye to one another, and Jonathan Jackson strode off to meet his limousine, briefcase in one hand, rumpled handkerchief still clutched in the other.

Lorinda and James put on their coats and collected their hand luggage. Then they looked at each other.

"Well," said Lorinda, "we got here in one piece. Or two pieces. And the plane stayed in the sky."

"And next . . ." said James.

"And next is Aunt Marian and six months full of question marks. Let's go, James."

4
Aunt Marian

"Well," Lorinda was to say to James later, "I have to admit that Uncle Harry and Aunt Marian did all the right things. As well as they know how, anyway."

They were there to meet them at the airport, Uncle Harry looking quiet and calm, Aunt Marian's face full of anxiety. She kept fidgeting with her purse clasp and turning her head right and left. "Even though," Lorinda pointed out, "there was only one door we could come through."

"Well," James argued, "you can't blame her if she didn't want to miss us. I wouldn't call it something *bad!*"

"Oh, I know, I know," said Lorinda. "It's just that she's so nervous."

"Well, Uncle Harry's not."

Lorinda laughed. "Uncle Harry's so silent he's three-quarters dead."

James sighed. "I wish he looked more like Daddy," he said, "being a brother and all. All the rest of

Daddy's family is skinny. I wonder how come he got to be so round and fat."

"You'd be round and fat too," said Lorinda, "if all you did was sit around looking kind of sad, watching TV or Aunt Marian. He doesn't even exercise his *vocal* chords."

But that all happened later. At the airport, they finally got their suitcases off the baggage conveyor belt and lugged them to the car.

"There's so *much*," said Aunt Marian, the line between her eyebrows deepening. "I just hope it'll all fit."

Lorinda was determined to be cheerful, at least for the first day. "As Mummy said, you have to be prepared for hot and cold, dry and wet. That adds up to a lot of stuff. After all, we're going to be here for six whole months."

"I know," said Aunt Marian, her voice dreary.

Well, thanks, thought Lorinda. Thanks a lot.

Conversation on the hundred and thirty kilometre ride to Peterborough was not very lively. Uncle Harry's repeated comment was, "Well, well, well," and Aunt Marian's contributions seemed to be rooted in pessimism.

"Do either of you get car sick? I've brought paper bags."

"No," said James, who, for the first time in his life, started to feel like he might.

"Well, well, well," said Uncle Harry.

"Buckle up," warned Aunt Marian. "They charge you fifty dollars if they catch you without a seat belt. Besides," she sighed, "there are accidents almost every single day on this stretch of the 401, and there's a lot of ice today."

"Just as well Jonathan Jackson isn't here," whispered Lorinda to James.

"What? What?" asked Aunt Marian. "It's rude to whisper."

"Sorry," said Lorinda. "I was just talking about a man on the plane who had airplane phobia."

"Well, I can certainly sympathize with him. If those big planes crash, there's nothing, absolutely *nothing* you can do to save yourself. I don't know what possessed your parents to send you that way."

Lorinda could feel her temper rising. It was one thing to say it was rude to whisper. It was another thing to criticize her parents.

"They sent us that way," she said stiffly, "because we had to get here before school opened. And so we could have New Year's Day at home. And so we could say goodbye to our friends. And because my dad says airplanes are safer than cars." So there, she thought savagely.

"Hm," said Aunt Marian.

"Well, well, well" said Uncle Harry.

For the rest of the trip they sat mostly in

silence. The driving was difficult and the going was slow. When they speeded up, Aunt Marian would say, "Not so fast, Harold."

She did ask a few questions. "Do you like school?" she asked James.

"Yes," he said.

"Well, I hope the Ontario standards won't be too high for you."

Lorinda's mouth opened, but James dug her in the ribs with his elbow.

Aunt Marian sighed again. "I do hope you'll be all right. I'm sure it'll be hard for you, starting in the middle of the year when everyone knows everybody else and all the friendships are formed."

"That's why we wanted to be here on the very first day of the term," said Lorinda, trying very hard to make her voice sound friendly but not succeeding too well.

Aunt Marian looked back nervously from the front seat. "Just remember, if anything really bad happens, you're to come to me at once."

"Anything bad?" James asked, clutching his paper bag.

"Oh, you know. Bullying, or name-calling, or stealing — that kind of thing."

Oh, wonderful, thought Lorinda. I can see that this six months is going to be just wonderful.

By the time they reached Peterborough, it was

five o'clock. Aunt Marian said to Uncle Harry, "Let's go to McDonald's and get hamburgers. This has been a hard day for everyone, and it will give me a little holiday from cooking." Then she added bleakly, "Which I'll be doing a lot of in the weeks to come."

Lorinda looked at the ceiling of the car. James stared at his lap. Uncle Harry said, "Now, now, Marian." This seemed to be his other favourite remark.

"At least," Lorinda was to say later, "that proved he was alive. I didn't like the idea of a corpse driving the car."

"I think he's shy or sad or something," James said. "I didn't say very much myself on the way home. Even *you* were pretty quiet — for you."

"Well, I figured that no matter what I said it would be either a tragedy or something to worry about. So the best thing was just to shut up."

They all felt better after hamburgers at McDonald's. Lorinda and James thanked their uncle and aunt and said how much they had enjoyed the meal.

"I suppose you don't have too many chances to eat out," said Aunt Marian. They didn't, but Lorinda certainly wasn't going to say so. "It's probably just as well. I hate to think of all those strangers breathing their flu germs on my food."

Lorinda suddenly saw the flu germs as small,

busy beetles chasing each other all over the newly swallowed hamburger in her stomach. "Holy smoke!" she exclaimed.

"What? Where?" said Aunt Marian, looking around nervously.

"I said *holy* smoke," said Lorinda. "I just never thought about it that way. Flu germs and all. To me, a hamburger is a treat."

To Lorinda's surprise, Aunt Marian reached over and patted her on the knee. "I'm glad you're happy. I just hope you stay that way. Six months is a long, long time."

Everyone sighed. All except Uncle Harry, who said, "Now, now, Marian."

* * *

When they reached 14 Summer Street, even Lorinda had to admit she was impressed. The house was a yellow brick split-level, warm, bright and spacious inside. Everything looked shiningly clean. White organdy curtains were on the living room windows, and there were deep squishy rugs everywhere. Even the basement rooms had soft carpets and pretty curtains.

Aunt Marian and Uncle Harry had their bedroom on the highest level. Lorinda and James were given rooms in the basement, each with a little desk and a mirrored bureau, along with a comfortable-looking bed and a small bedside table. In the main part of the basement there was a huge empty closet for them to hang their clothes in, and a large cupboard with shelves for books, skates and precious belongings.

The rest of the house didn't matter to Lorinda after she saw that basement. It was all theirs. A private place, somewhere to escape to if things got too awful. Impulsively she turned to Aunt Marian and threw her arms around her. "Oh, thank you, *thank you!*" she almost yelled.

Aunt Marian stood stiff and confused in Lorinda's arms. Then she gave her a couple of little pats on the back. "For what? For what in particular?" she asked.

"For the basement. For giving us a special place."

"Yes," said James.

Uncle Harry was smiling. "Well, well, well," he said.

Later, when they were downstairs unpacking, Lorinda said, "Do you know why this place is such a lifesaver for us?"

"Sure," said James. "We can talk down here. We can complain out loud and no one will hear but the walls and the furnace. It's all our own. Nobody else is here. It's almost like a place to — hide."

At nine o'clock, Aunt Marian appeared at the door to the basement.

"Time for bed," she called down. "You should get lots of rest. Tomorrow is bound to be a very difficult day for you."

"Another cheerful message from the management," laughed Lorinda after the door closed.

But then she stopped laughing. Aunt Marian's words came floating back to her, nagging at her peace of mind. "Everybody knows everybody else . . . bullies . . . name-calling . . . stealing." She sighed.

"C'mon, James," she said. "She's probably right. It's been kind of a long day." She thought about waking up that morning, watching the lobster boats leave Blue Harbour, bright in the morning sun. She thought of the gulls riding still and silent on the cold waves. She remembered how Jessie's firm little body had felt when she hugged her. It seemed a million years ago. "Let's go to bed."

"All right," agreed James. He smiled. "Let's get ready for our very difficult day."

They both laughed. Then they were silent as they stared at one another. Even Aunt Marian couldn't have looked more worried than they did.

5
First day at school

Lorinda and James both woke up before their alarms went off. James usually padded around half asleep in the morning, without glasses — "like a zombie," his father often said — happy and dreamy in his own personal fog. But today he was wide awake and his glasses were firmly in place.

"C'mon, Lorinda," he said to the face peering out at him from under the covers. "Let's go upstairs and look outside. The windows down here are all frosted up and it was too dark to see anything last night."

Together they crept carefully up the stairs, noting that, unlike at home, none of them creaked. Softly they made their way to the living room, where a giant picture window faced the street.

"Wow!" breathed James. "Just look, Lorinda!"

"Jeepers!" whispered Lorinda. "It's not Blue Harbour, but if it can look like this even once in a while, it can't be all bad."

The snow outside was deep and fresh. It clung

to the trees, the roofs, even the telephone lines. The sky was just starting to lighten. It was going to be a clear, bright day.

The scene in front of them looked just like a picture on a Christmas card. Lorinda and James pressed against the glass and gazed out in silence. As their breath steamed up the window, they rubbed it off.

"Good morning," said a cool, polite voice. They turned to see Aunt Marian in a deep blue velour robe, her hair as perfect as it had been at the airport.

Lorinda's hand went up to her own tangled tresses. "How on earth —" she began.

"Please, children," interrupted their aunt, standing stiffly on the threshold, "try to keep your hands off the windows. I know you don't want to make extra work for me, wiping off smudges. Look at the marks. What were you going to say, Lorinda? You said, 'How on earth,' and then stopped."

"Oh, nothing much," said Lorinda. She had been going to ask how Aunt Marian managed to have such beautiful hair after sleeping on it all night, but she didn't feel like asking anymore. Instead, she looked at the window and saw what a mess she and James had made of it. "Sorry," she said. "It was just that it looked so pretty outside."

Aunt Marian smiled. "It does, doesn't it? But it

will look just as pretty if you stand away from the window." She paused. "Do you have slippers?"

"Yes."

"Well, do wear them, then. I don't want you getting needles or pins in your feet. Besides, I don't feel it's too healthy to go without shoes."

James thought about how often they went barefoot in the summer at home, walking over gravel roads, climbing on sharp, uneven rocks, kicking through the dust. "I like the feel of your carpets between my toes," he said.

Aunt Marian smiled again. "Well, I suppose it *is* kind of a treat for you."

Lorinda knew she should have said, "Yes, it's a wonderful treat," because it was. She would never stop loving those carpets. But instead, she felt angry. Aunt Marian had visited their house in Blue Harbour two summers ago. She must remember they had nothing but bare, painted floors with hooked mats on them. Lorinda felt like a poor relation. Which I am, she thought.

Someone coughed and they looked up to see Uncle Harry coming down the hall wearing a red plaid dressing gown. "Well, well, well!" he greeted them. "Good morning!"

Two new words, thought Lorinda. "Hi, Uncle Harry," she said, glad to forget carpets for a minute. "Is it always this gorgeous in Ontario?"

"Well, sort of," he chuckled. Why, maybe Uncle Harry was going to be *nice*. "That is to say, it's piled full of snow most of the time here in Peterborough. Toronto is more drizzly and damp, like your part of the world."

Lorinda's brows came together and she took a deep breath. Before she could speak, James gave her a poke. "Most of the time?" he asked, hoping Lorinda could calm herself before she spoiled everything.

"Yep," said Uncle Harry. "Sometimes the snow never leaves from the end of November to the first of April. By the middle of March, most people around here would welcome some of that Nova Scotia mildness. It's just white, white, white, week after week."

Lorinda relaxed. "Great for coasting or skiing, though," she said.

Aunt Marian coughed. "I've made you a big nourishing breakfast. You'd better hurry and eat it, so you can get to school a bit early today. You'll need to see the principal and arrange things." She paused. "Would you feel better if I went with you? You may find it pretty strange."

"No! No! No!" exclaimed Lorinda. We wouldn't need to feel better, she thought to herself, if you'd just stop telling us how terrible it's going to be — and what we don't need is some grown-up trailing along on our very first day. "We'll be *fine*," she continued out loud. "We're used to doing things on our own."

"Then hurry!" Aunt Marian clapped her hands. "You don't want to be late and annoy the principal on the very first morning."

"Now, now, Marian," said Uncle Harry.

*   *   *

Downstairs, Lorinda pulled on her best sweater and jeans, and brushed her long black hair till it shone. She looked at herself in the mirror and shrugged her shoulders. James arrived at her door dressed in his Nova Scotia plaid shirt and a brand new pair of jeans. His hair, as always, looked as though he had been out in the wind.

"We both look good," said Lorinda.

"We'll be fine. City people aren't *that* much different from us, are they? And Ontario isn't *China*, after all. It's not on the other side of the world."

"Right!" agreed Lorinda.

Neither of them felt like eating. They were too excited or uneasy or *something*. But they pressed on through half a grapefruit, oatmeal porridge, a boiled egg (too runny), and toast. Better to feel stuffed, they agreed when Aunt Marian was out of the room, than to hear a lecture on gratitude or health.

"Thank you for the big breakfast," said Lorinda when they had finished.

"Yes."

"Well," said Aunt Marian, with a little sigh, "I must say they've taught you to be very polite." Then, "Are you sure jeans are what you should be wearing to school?"

Oh, Aunt Marian, wailed Lorinda inside her head, if I live with you long enough, I'm not going to feel sure about anything at all.

"Yes," she said firmly, "I'm sure." But she wasn't, not anymore.

"Well, I do hope you're right," said Aunt Marian, sighing yet again. "I'd just hate for you to feel out of place on your first day."

By now they were dressed in their outdoor clothes. "Let's get outa here," muttered Lorinda to James, and they rushed out the door, yelling goodbye over their shoulders.

"James," growled Lorinda, "that woman has got me so snarled up I can't even enjoy this snow. It's the most beautiful stuff I ever saw, and yet right now I don't care if it's all melted by tonight."

"Which," said James, "it's not gonna be till April. Lookit, Lorinda, I know she's a pain, but she's not a real *ogre*. It's not like she *whips* us or anything. She's just kind of . . ."

"Chilly."

"Yes. And sort of . . ."

"Nervous."

"Yes. And . . ."

"Clean and perfect."

"Yes. Well," he sighed, "those aren't really *crimes*."

"Oh, James!" Lorinda kicked a hunk of snow till it hit a garbage can. "You make me so *mad!* I wish you wouldn't always look on the doggone bright side of everything. I wish you weren't so darn *fair*. I bet if a criminal came and kidnapped Jessie, you'd say the man was mean because his mother had spanked him a lot when he was a kid."

James laughed so hard he tripped and fell headfirst into a snowdrift. "Maybe that'd be the reason," he said as he brushed himself off. "But if anyone kidnapped Jessie, I'd chase him till I caught him. Then I'd throw him into one of the boiling bark-pots back home, along with the nets. By the time he was fished out he'd look like a stewed prune. And he'd be covered all over with markings from the nets, like a waffle."

They turned a corner, and there was the school. No one had told them it would be so enormous. It was as big as a hospital — or a penitentiary. There had to be about a million kids. Some of them were coasting down a big hill at the back on pieces of cardboard, green garbage bags, the seats of their pants — shrieking and laughing.

James watched, eyes bulging behind his glasses. "Neat!" he breathed.

"C'mon," ordered Lorinda. "Like Aunt Marian said, we gotta keep this principal guy happy."

* * *

The principal wasn't anything to be frightened of at all. He told them to sit down and welcomed them to Ontario. He asked a few questions about their school work in Nova Scotia, and even some things about the weather and fishing and the scenery. He didn't panic when the bell rang, either. He seemed really interested in everything they had to say. Then he mentioned that when he was a kid he'd dreamed of being a sailor and going to sea. "And your father goes to sea every day of his life," he added wistfully.

"When he's well enough," corrected James.

"Yes. Right. But that winter in Texas is bound to fix him up right as rain."

Lorinda told James later that it was the first time in her life she'd wanted to throw her arms around a principal and hug him.

"But now," said the principal, whose name was Mr. Archibald, "we'd better deliver you to your classrooms before the whole morning is gone. And remember," he added, his face serious, "if you have any questions or problems, or things you need to talk about, I want you to feel free to come to me."

"Thanks," they said.

When Mr. Archibald took James to his classroom, Lorinda was close enough behind to see what went on. With his hands on James' shoulders, the principal introduced "the new boy from Nova Scotia" and said he was sure everyone would do all they could to help him feel at home. The teacher looked young and pretty. When Mr. Archibald came out without James and closed the door behind him, Lorinda felt abandoned.

"Now," he said, "it's your turn."

Yes, thought Lorinda, if I can just survive to tell the tale.

They climbed a long wide set of stairs to the second floor, where Mr. Archibald stopped outside Room 23 and knocked.

"Come in!" called a man's deep voice.

Mr. Archibald opened the door.

6
Mildred

Lorinda thought she would faint when she saw her teacher. She'd never had a man teacher before. He was so tall, he looked like a giant. He reminded her of her favourite hockey player, only he was bigger. In her confusion, she couldn't remember the player's name.

"Mr. O'Reilly, this is Lorinda," Mr. Archibald was saying. "She's from Nova Scotia. She'll be with us for the rest of the year. Here's her file." He turned to the class. "I know you'll all make her feel welcome."

Lorinda looked at the roomful of faces. There were twenty-seven of them. And I don't know a single one, she thought. Not one. I'm going to be taught by Wayne Gretzky — she'd just remembered his name — which is scary enough, but I wish I could go someplace where I didn't have to face all these strange kids. Well, at least they're wearing jeans. That's *one* good thing.

But Lorinda didn't let any of her thoughts

show. She shook Mr. O'Reilly's hand and faced the class with her head up. He was speaking. At first she didn't understand what he was saying, but then she heard, "Class, I want you to meet Lorinda. Lorinda Dauphinee." He was pronouncing her name "Dough-fee-nay."

Oh, my gosh, thought Lorinda, I can't make a spectacle of myself on the very first morning by correcting him. What if I make him mad? But she couldn't keep herself from saying, "I'm sorry, Mr. O'Reilly . . ."

Mr. O'Reilly stopped, puzzled. "What's that, Lorinda?"

"I'm sorry, but that's not the way you say my name. I know it's *right* because it's a French name and all. But . . ."

"But?"

"On the South Shore of Nova Scotia, they call it something else."

"Which is?"

"Doff-nee."

To her relief, Mr. O'Reilly smiled. "Then that's what you'll be. We'll start again. Class, this is Lorinda *Doff-nee*. She's from one of the Atlantic Provinces." He walked over to the map on one wall. "Here." He pointed to the tiny peninsula on the east coast of Canada. "Lots of water, I guess," he said with a grin.

"Yes," Lorinda replied, "lots."

The desks were arranged in a sort of horseshoe. Mr. O'Reilly showed Lorinda hers. She was between two other girls — Sarah Cohen and Mildred Walker, she found out later. There were notebooks and pencils laid out all ready for her.

"It's math this period," whispered Sarah. "Are you any good at it?"

Lorinda was very good at math. She didn't know what to answer. "Okay," she said. "I guess I'm okay."

The math was easy, and Mr. O'Reilly praised her work. He seemed to be doing all he could to make her feel at home in his class.

The first part of the morning passed quickly, and before long the recess bell rang. Now I know I'm going to die, thought Lorinda. She stood up and tried to look as busy as the rest of them, putting things away inside her almost empty desk, straightening pencils.

"Sarah and Mildred," said Wayne Gretzky, coming up behind them, "perhaps you'll show Lorinda the ropes today, okay?"

"Okay."

Out in the schoolyard, the girls walked up and down near the swings to keep warm.

"Lorinda's a funny name," said Mildred. "Where'd you get it?"

Lorinda felt herself tighten. "It was my grand-mother's name," she replied. She could see James flying down the hill on a piece of cardboard. She wished he was here. Or that she was there. She didn't want James to *do* anything. She just wanted him standing nearby, looking calm.

"What on earth do people do for a living in Nova Scotia? It looks so *small*." Mildred again.

"It *is* small. It's almost an island. It has sea all around it, and hills and rocks and beaches. People do lots of things. Daddy's a fisherman."

"A *what?*"

"A fisherman."

"Well, what does he do?"

What a dumb question. "He catches fish. He paints his boat and fixes the engine. He mends nets. Makes lobster traps."

"My dad's a doctor."

"Uh-huh." Lorinda thought of saying, "Well, what does he do?"

It was Sarah's turn to speak. "My Aunt Esther went to Nova Scotia on her honeymoon. She says it's beautiful."

Lorinda knew for sure she was going to like Sarah.

"She's right. It *is* beautiful." Then she paused and looked at Sarah. "I'm only here until July," she said, "because Daddy's sick. He had to go someplace warm. Maybe some summer you can come and visit." She laughed. "Or maybe you could come on your honeymoon."

"I'm sorry your dad's sick," said Sarah.

"Do you really call your father Daddy?" asked Mildred. "*Still?*"

Lorinda was hanging onto her temper by her fingernails. "And why not?" she retorted. "Mummy says that —"

"And *Mummy!*"

"Yes. What's wrong with that?"

"Nothing, I guess. If you happen to be just a little kid."

"Lay off, eh, Mildred?" said Sarah. "It's tough to be new."

"You're telling me!" exclaimed Mildred. "I was new myself last year. No one was falling all over themselves welcoming *me*."

"Start being friendly yourself for just half a day," said Sarah, "and we might start welcoming you even now." Then she grabbed Lorinda by the arm and pulled her away, leaving Mildred standing alone in the field.

Lorinda sighed. "I've only been in this school two hours and I've made an enemy already."

Sarah laughed. "Well, you aren't the first enemy Mildred's made, that's for sure. Try not to let her get you down. She's been trying to find a friend ever since she hit this place, but she goes at it all backwards."

James came racing up to them, covered with snow. Beside him was another boy — blond, sturdy, tough-looking. "Hi, Lorinda!" yelled James. "What a great hill! This is my friend Hank. This is my sister Lorinda. Hank lent me his cardboard. Wanna try the hill?"

But the bell rang and it was time to go in — to sit beside Mildred Walker again. Oh, well. Sarah would be on the other side.

Back in the classroom, Mr. O'Reilly announced that they were going to talk about this term's teams. He wrote on the board: *BASKETBALL — HOCKEY — SOCCER — GYMNASTICS*.

"Now," he said, "who wants to volunteer for the tryouts? They're tomorrow at four o'clock, at the rink behind the school and in the gym. If there's a team you're interested in, hold up your hand."

Lorinda watched all the hands shoot up. Then slowly, shyly, she put up her own hand.

"Lorinda, what team do you want to try out for?"

"Hockey," she said.

There was silence followed by a giggle or two. Then Mr. O'Reilly said, "There's no rule about girls not being allowed to play hockey. I don't think so, anyway. But this is the first time a girl has ever asked. Have you played before?"

"Yes."

"On a team?"

"Yes."

"I don't want you to get hurt by a bunch of rough boys, Lorinda, so I'll have to ask you. Are you good?"

Lorinda didn't say anything for a moment. She knew she was good, but she didn't want to make everyone mad by sounding like a boaster. "Why don't you let me try out for the team, and then you can decide?" she said.

Mr. O'Reilly laughed. "Good idea," he said. "Okay, I'll check it out with the coach, and if everything's all right, you can try out at the rink at four o'clock tomorrow. You're sure you wouldn't like to try gymnastics or basketball?"

"I never did gymnastics, and I can't play basketball. Besides, they both look kinda slow to me."

"Well, let's wait and see what happens," suggested Mr. O'Reilly.

After that, the day passed quickly. In the afternoon, they did grammar and composition, and that was okay. Lorinda always enjoyed making up stories. Then they had social studies, during which Mr. O'Reilly showed a film about the pioneers of the Peterborough district. When the projector broke down, he went off to find someone to fix it, and the kids made the same racket and threw the same kind of paper airplanes as they did back in Nova Scotia. Lorinda shot an airplane off herself. It landed in the overhead lighting fixture.

Then Mr. O'Reilly returned with a handyman he'd found changing light bulbs in the staff room. The man tinkered with the projector for about fifteen minutes, turning the light on and off, muttering to himself under his breath, tightening things with his screwdriver. At last he admitted that he was new on the job and he didn't know much about that kind of machine.

At that, Mr. O'Reilly said, "All right, class. Since it's the first day of school anyway, I don't think the world will come to an end if I let you out ten minutes early." Everyone cheered. Not so bad, thought Lorinda. Apart from Mildred.

On their way home, Sarah said to Lorinda, "I'm a Jew, you know."

"So?"

"So I thought you might like to know."

"Sure. Well, I guess so."

"Do you know what a Jew is?"

"Oh, someone who's part of some group. Like an Irishman. Or an African. Or a Nova Scotian, even. Is that right?"

"Well, not exactly," said Sarah. "You can be an Irishman or a Nova Scotian and still be a Jew too."

"Well, what is it then? We don't have a single one where I live. Is it special?"

"Oh, yes," Sarah grinned. "But sometimes hard."

"Why hard?"

"Oh, I dunno. Sometimes you feel outside things, unless you're with other Jews. Like at Christmas time. We don't have Christmas. And sometimes, without doing a single thing wrong, people don't like you. Can you imagine what that's like?"

"I don't have to imagine. Aunt Marian doesn't like me very much, and I haven't done anything except just *be* here. And I have to live with Aunt Marian. Mildred isn't exactly in love with me, either. And I sure don't feel like I belong here."

Sarah turned to Lorinda. "Let's be best friends while you're here. You can come over to my place whenever you want. My mom'll make you feel better when you get homesick or anything."

Lorinda smiled, "I bet with a good friend like you, Aunt Marian and Mildred Walker won't bother me any more than a couple of mosquito bites."

But as she walked toward 14 Summer Street after Sarah left, Lorinda knew this wasn't true. Or if it was true, those mosquito bites were badly infected. They didn't just itch. They hurt.

7

Letters

On January 12, Lorinda and James came home to find a letter addressed to them. Lorinda opened it with shaking fingers.

She read out loud.

Dear Lorinda and James,

Jessie and Daddy and I arrived safely at Uncle John's yesterday, and we are all fine. Uncle John, as you know, is a whole lot older than we are and I suppose you'd think he is a funny old bachelor. He's been getting his own meals for years and years, so he's kind of pleased to have a cook in the house (me). He and Dad play crib in the evenings, and that makes him happy too.

We live on a ranch — which is really a farmhouse (not very big) with a lot of land. There are cows and horses and all sorts of animals to keep Jessie happy. I like them too — even the pigs, most of all the little ones. The two hired men sleep above the barn and get their own meals in a shed that's built on to it out there. We have a bedroom looking out over the fields. Jessie sleeps on a cot in the upper hall in a sort of jog. There's a curtain across it and she's very proud of her own room. But she misses you both.

It's warm and dry here. I hope your father will soon feel better. We miss you a whole lot and wish you were with us. I've already sent Lorinda's gift for her birthday, even though it's over a month away.

Jessie sends a hug to both of you and so does your father. Write us lots of letters so we won't be too lonesome for you.

Say hello and thank you for us to Uncle Harry and Aunt Marian. It's very kind of them to have you as their guests, because they're not used to children. It will be a big adjustment for them. I know I can count on you to be helpful and co-operative.

Be sure to wear lots of clothes when it's cold. You'll need those warm wool socks I made you.

I love you both an awful lot,
Mummy

P.S. Here's a letter from Jessie.

"You're sweet happy tootin' they're not used to children," muttered Lorinda to James when she'd finished reading the letter aloud. "Look what happened when you brought Hank here after soccer practice yesterday. You'd have thought he was one of those criminals from the *WANTED* signs in the post office. Your very best friend!"

"I know," sighed James. "But you have to admit he's pretty wild looking. His hair makes you think he sleeps standing on his head, and he looks like he hasn't changed his sweater for a month, which he probably hasn't. You know Aunt Marian. If you're not clean, you can't be worth much."

"Oh, well," said Lorinda, "let's not think about it anymore. We've got an hour before supper. Why don't we each write a letter to the family? They might be almost as lonely as we are."

So they got some lined paper out of their school loose-leafs and set to work.

January 12

Dear Mummy and Daddy and Jessie,

Lorinda and I got your letter. Thanks. I wish I was there. I'd like to see all those animals too. I miss Petunia. I know she's an old cow, but she's ours. I hope Mr. Hyson doesn't forget to feed her.

Here it is cold. We have snow all the time. We coast down the hill at school on cardboard. Hank is my best friend. He's teaching me how to wrestle. His father taught him how. You have to get the other guy down on the ground so he can't move. Can he come visit us in Blue Harbour? I hope Daddy gets well soon. I think Aunt Marian tries to be nice. Uncle Harry is friendly but doesn't say a lot. I'm reading a good book from the school library. I never wrote a letter this long before. Lorinda helped me with the spelling. Hank has four brothers and two sisters. Write soon. XXX.

Love
James

Jan. 12

Dear Mummy and Daddy and Jessie,

Thank you for the nice letter. It was good to hear about the farm but it made me sad too. Because I'm not there. But we're fine. Don't worry about us. Aunt Marian cooks really good stuff and she always asks if we're warm enough.

We have two rooms all our own in the basement. We can go down there when we're tired of being polite. I didn't know being polite could be so tiring.

Peterborough is nice. It has snow all the time. Sarah lends me a sled for coasting on the school hill. She says her brother will let me borrow his skis sometime so I can learn to ski. Sarah is a Jew. A Jew is someone special. But sometimes people are unkind to them for no reason. It must be like Mr. Collicut hating Catholics, even though he once told me he never met one. Sometimes people are so stupid. Mildred is mean to me sometimes for no reason. She says I talk funny. That's because I talk Nova Scotian instead of Ontarian. It sounds a lot the same to me, but she's pretty picky. She says my winter coat is too long. I told her that's because it has to last a long time. Sarah says my coat is fine. She says Mildred is mean to me because I'm new and almost an orphan. That makes me special. And Mr. O'Reilly is extra nice to me so I'll feel happy. Mildred is in love with Mr. O'Reilly, who is exactly like Wayne Gretzky, only taller, and he doesn't teach school on skates!

Uncle Harry is nice but he doesn't talk much. I think Aunt Marian is the boss in this house. When she is too much of a pain all he says is "Now, now, Marian." I know what *I'd* say to her if she was my wife. But I don't own her like I own you guys and James. So mostly I'm polite and quiet. She's not mean or anything (or so James says). She just needs to be dumped in a summer camp or an orphanage for a while to find out what kids are really like.

I tried out for the hockey team and I did real good. But the coach has to decide if he'll let a girl on the team.

Mildred lost her good silver pen with her name on it the very first day I came to school. When she reported it, she kept looking at me like I was the thief. I hope it's not a sinful thing to do, but I keep praying every night that Mildred's father will get sick or transferred or something and have to leave Peterborough.

Everything is just fine here. Don't worry about us.

Could you send a picture of all of you? I forgot to bring one. We need two, one for each room, and maybe an extra one for my wallet.

Love and kisses and bear hugs,
Lorinda.

Lorinda's next letter was to Duncan.

Dear Duncan,
Here I am in Ontario. It has lakes instead

of the sea. I like the sea better, but this is pretty good. One thing about it, there is a lot of snow — in Peterborough, anyway. It's real pretty. It snows so often it always looks clean and bright. I sound like Aunt Marian! Clean and bright is what she wants everything to be. She's full of instructions. She almost never just *talks*. You know, like saying, "How is your friend Sarah?" or, "How do you feel about hockey?" She's too busy telling us not to fall through the ice or not to catch cold or not to drop crumbs on the carpet. James says she can't help it, but you know James. He'd say it wasn't the Devil's fault for making Hell so hot. Sarah's mother is like a second mother to me. Sarah is my best friend. (Just for here. You're my best-ever best friend.) Her mother hugs me when she thinks I need it, and even if I don't.

Our school is called Duke of York. Is it ever huge. Mildred is awful. She sits next to me in school. She is real smart, which just makes it worse. She tries to make out I'm a *villain*. She tells everyone I look funny and talk funny, and even acts like I stole her stupid pen. It's got her name on it. So even if she *gave* it to me I'd throw it into the Trent Canal. I could wring her neck.

I've tried out for the hockey team, but

maybe they won't take me because I'm a girl. What a drag.

Write soon.

I wish I could walk on the beach and skate on Granite Pond with all the kids. I don't tell Mummy and Daddy, but I'm so homesick I could die.

Love,
Lorinda.

8
Coach Zomer's decision

The next couple of weeks were difficult ones for Lorinda. James seemed to be fine. He spent most of his free time with Hank, and every day he went off to school with his own piece of cardboard for coasting down the hill at recess. Uncle Harry had cut it off an old carton for him. He told him to keep it in the garage so Aunt Marian wouldn't worry about the seat of his pants.

But for Lorinda, life was not such plain sailing. More and more things were disappearing from the school, and it couldn't all be just carelessness. People often remembered exactly where they had left the items — watches, rings, jack-knives, even expensive things from the staff room. Mildred had a lot to say about this — mostly in a loud voice.

"My dad says he never expected a child of his would have to go to a school where there were *thieves*," she announced one day at recess. "At first he was mad at me for losing my pen. It was a gift from my grandmother and it's *sterling silver*. But when I told him I knew *exactly* where I left it and *what happened*, then he wasn't angry anymore. Or not at *me*, anyway."

"Wadda ya mean, what happened?" someone asked.

"You know," Mildred said, looking smug and pitiful all at the same time. "The lights kept going off and on that afternoon because of the social studies film and all. A person could have taken it without anyone seeing or knowing. You remember that day. It was the time the projector broke down — the day we chose what teams to try out for — the first day of the new term — the day Lorinda arrived." Mildred looked sideways at Lorinda, and then she said, "The thief'd have to be very quiet to take it off my desk — and *close by*."

Lorinda wanted to scream, "Stop accusing me! I never took your dumb silver pen!" But she was smart enough not to draw attention to herself. She just gritted her teeth hard and pretended she hadn't heard.

The other big thing Lorinda had to worry about (apart from trying to please Aunt Marian all the time and never quite succeeding) was the hockey coach's decision. The coach, Mr. Zomer, was having a hard time making up his mind. "I know she's good," he said one day to Mr. O'Reilly in the staff room. "Very good, in fact. She moves like the wind and she seems strong. She's accurate in her passing and shooting too."

"Well, then?" prompted Mr. O'Reilly.

"Well, I dunno. She's a girl. Maybe she can't stand up to the rough stuff. On a team, you have to be able to depend on strength. And you don't want any awful accidents. But —"

"Go on."

"But I hate to see the kid unhappy. She loves hockey so much I think she must dream about it every night. I thought girls only liked dolls and clothes."

Mr. O'Reilly laughed. "Oh, come on, Al! Where've you been all your life? Lorinda would trade a doll for a hockey stick any day. Why not give her a break?"

Mr. Zomer fiddled with his whistle and stared into space for a moment or two. Then he got out of his chair and walked up and down the staff room. After a few minutes he sighed. "Tell you what," he said to Mr. O'Reilly. "I'll compromise. We practise four times a week. I'll tell her she can come and play with the team once a week. That'll keep her skills polished for when she's back home next year, and I won't feel like such a dragon. But —"

"But what?"

"She can't be on the team. I've decided. No. She definitely can't. I won't risk it. She might get hurt in one of the inter-school games. They can get pretty rough."

When the coach gave this news to Lorinda, she felt like lifting her hockey stick and shooting it right across the ice into the boards. She was dying to say, "Thanks, Mr. Zomer, but if you don't want me on the team, don't try giving me any booby prizes. Playing with the team once a week will make me feel worse, not better. No thanks. I'll stay home and maybe embroider a pillow slip."

But all she said was, "Okay, Mr. Zomer. I'll be there on Fridays at four."

The day after the coach told Lorinda his decision, she and James each wrote a letter. James wrote to Glynis.

Dear Glynis,

I know you can't read this because you haven't learned how yet. Ask your mom or dad to read it. You're two years younger than me but very old in the head. You're my best friend in Blue Harbour. I miss you. I have a new best friend here. His name is Hank. He comes from the poor part of town and is very strong and tough. This is good for me because no one will bully you if Hank is your best friend. He swears and stuff like that, but he is kind. He also thinks of fun things to do. I don't care how he talks or that his face is dirty. Aunt Marian never had any kids, so she's peculiar. Think of me when you're on your Thinking Rock.

Love,
James

P.S. Lorinda says hi. She helps me with the hard words.

Lorinda wrote to Duncan.

Dear Duncan,
How are you?
I'm so mad I could spit. Yesterday the hockey coach decided to keep me off the team. He said I might get hurt. He said hockey is too rough for girls. Last night I was ready to pack my suitcase and go back to Blue Harbour and live in the barn with Petunia. Aunt Marian wasn't any help. When I told her about it, she said, "I'm so relieved. I was lying awake worrying about it. Sometimes people lose their front teeth playing hockey."

James said that the fact she was so worried about my safety that she couldn't sleep was a sign Aunt Marian likes me. But she probably just doesn't feel she should return me to Mummy and Daddy without any teeth.

Anyway I was too mad at everybody to think or care.

Say hi to Fiona and George and Glynis.

Love,
Lorinda

P.S. Someone stole a gold ring from Miss Hennessey's desk drawer today. Mildred keeps saying that everything started disappearing the day I arrived. Sarah says not to worry, but I do. I don't want to spend the rest of the year in jail for something I didn't do. Or wherever they put girls who are almost eleven years old who are accused of stealing things. Mostly I hate it that maybe people are looking at me and wondering.

9

Lorinda gets mad

From the beginning, Lorinda knew it was going to be a terrible day. Right after she got out of bed, she tripped over her geography book and stubbed her toe. Then she broke her only comb on a big tangle and went to breakfast with her hair in a mess. Aunt Marian said she couldn't go to school looking like that, and that her hair wasn't even very clean.

Breakfast was very thin porridge, which Lorinda hated. Uncle Harry went off to work without even saying goodbye, and when James asked if he could go to Hank's house for supper, Aunt Marian said no because Hank lived in a slummy part of town.

"Who knows what germs might be in the food?" she said, twisting her hands together and furrowing her brow. "In places like that, there's often a lot of rough behaviour. Maybe someone drunk. No. I'm afraid you can't go."

It was then that Lorinda broke wide open. A

whole month of politeness and control exploded into the kitchen.

"You stop that, Aunt Marian!" she yelled.

Aunt Marian's face tightened up as though someone had turned a knob, hard, on her forehead, and she clutched her fingers together. But she didn't say a word while Lorinda let fly with all her boxed-in fury.

"My hair looks like this because I broke my comb, and I only have one. That's because I'm not rich and don't have six combs. And my hair's not dirty, I washed it last night. I just don't happen to have been born with beautiful, perfect, tidy hair like yours."

She took a deep breath, but she had no intention of stopping. "And Hank! How can you say his home will be bad just because he's poor? The Blue Harbour Dauphinees are poor, but that doesn't make us bad people. You'd be really lucky if you had a friend like Hank. Every school in the world has got bullies in it. Hank *protects* James. He's very warm-hearted and that's a whole lot more important than being clean or tidy, or even being safe and hanging on to your front teeth!"

Lorinda knew she'd said some pretty awful things. She figured that Aunt Marian would send her home now anyway (where? where was home?), so she went right on yelling.

"I know it's kind of you to have us staying with you for six months. I know you don't really like children, so it must be awful. I know my bedroom is your old sewing room. I know you must be mad at me every time you want to sew on a button. And we're grateful. But I'm so tired of being grateful. I'm sick out of my skin of being grateful. I hope I never have to be grateful for anything else, ever, for the rest of my life. And I'm nearly crazy in the head from trying to be well-behaved every minute of the day."

Then Lorinda turned around. She couldn't bear to look at Aunt Marian's eyes. She didn't know what message she would read there. All the fizz had gone out of her, and she was already ashamed of what she'd done.

"I'm sorry, Aunt Marian," she choked out. "I'm really and truly sorry if I've made you mad or sad. Probably both. This is a nice house, and you and Uncle Harry aren't mean or anything. You cook real good meals and wash our clothes and keep us safe. But I just miss so much being *loved*."

Lorinda gave a big shuddering sob, but she didn't really cry. She couldn't, because it was time to leave for school. But she sat down at the foot of the stairs and moaned, "Oh! I wish you had a cow!"

Finally Aunt Marian spoke. Her voice came out tight and cold. "A cow?"

76

"Petunia," explained James. "Our cow."

"But a *cow!*" said Aunt Marian.

"Yes," said James. "A cow is something big and warm and furry that you can love and hug. She doesn't ask for anything. She just stands there and gives you what you need. When I'm sad, I often go out to the barn and sit with Petunia. I look at her big calm brown eyes and I touch her soft body. Sometimes that's all it takes to make me feel better." He thought for a moment, then added, "Often animals are more comforting than people."

When Lorinda passed Aunt Marian on the way out the door, she still couldn't look into her eyes. But she managed to speak. "Aunt Marian?"

"Yes?"

"I'll try not to do that again. I didn't feel it coming on, or maybe I could've stopped it."

But James looked at Aunt Marian hard before he followed Lorinda out the door. Then he reached out with his hand and touched her on the arm.

"You could use a cow yourself, right now," he said.

* * *

At school, things were no better. Sarah was away with a cold, so Lorinda had to spend the day with Mildred and an empty seat.

"Going to the hockey game this afternoon?" asked Mildred from behind her notebook.

Rub it in, thought Lorinda. Be sure to rub it in good and hard. "No," she said.

"Duke of York is playing Dominion School," Mildred went on. "If you don't go, people will think you're mad about not being on the team. Nobody likes a poor sport."

Then why have you devoted your whole entire life to being one? thought Lorinda. "Maybe you're right," she sighed. "Okay, I'll go."

"Want to go with me?" asked Mildred.

What could Lorinda say? Sarah was sick. Hank and James were going together, and she hadn't made arrangements to go with anyone else. She couldn't just say, "Thanks, but no thanks."

"Okay," said Lorinda.

"Meet you on the corner of Monaghan Road at four."

"I can't figure it out," said Lorinda to James on the way home to lunch. "Why did she want me to go with her?"

"Well" — James scratched his head under his toque — "could be lots of things. Maybe she plans to do something mean this afternoon. But maybe not. Maybe she wishes you were her friend instead of Sarah's. Maybe she's jealous."

"Time will tell," said Lorinda. "I'm ready for anything today. Bad or good, I hardly care which."

But she did care which. When she got home for lunch, she was so embarrassed about seeing Aunt Marian that she raced right downstairs without watching what she was doing and bumped into a table in the basement hall. A small vase fell off and smashed into a hundred pieces on the floor.

As Lorinda picked up the pieces with shaking fingers, she wondered if anything else bad could happen that day. She stood up, her hands full of broken china, and there was Aunt Marian at the bottom of the stairs.

"Oh, Aunt Marian," she gasped, "I could just die. I'll pay for it. I really will. Even if it takes me twenty years to earn the money."

"You can't," said Aunt Marian. "It's an antique. You can't replace it." Her face was blank, a mask. "There's nowhere you could buy one like it. It doesn't matter. Put the pieces in the waste basket. Don't cut your fingers. Your lunch is ready."

"If I don't cry, I'm going to bust wide open," said Lorinda in a shaky voice to James. "So you go have lunch and try to explain to Aunt Marian that I can't come."

Then she went into her bedroom, threw herself down on the pretty spread, and cried hard for ten minutes. When she was finished, she went upstairs, red-eyed and silent, and choked down the egg sandwich that Aunt Marian had prepared. "Thank you," she whispered, and left for school.

* * *

The afternoon was no better. There was a report on another theft, this time of a wristwatch that had been left in the girls' washroom. Lorinda had been in the washroom in the morning and several people knew this. She had nine spelling mistakes in her composition, but Mr. O'Reilly said it was the best in the class. "Wouldn't surprise me if you ended up a big author," he said.

"Teacher's pet!" said Mildred, in a whisper everyone could hear.

But Mildred was there on the corner at four o'clock, waiting, and she and Lorinda went up to the rink together. Now that they were alone, Mildred was friendly — to Lorinda, anyway. At one point she said, "We could be really good friends if it wasn't for Sarah. What do you want to be friends with *her* for?"

"Because I like her. Because she's kind. Because she doesn't say mean things — like some other people do."

"Well, I think she's stupid. Sometimes she gets low marks in math."

"Low marks don't matter."

"And I bet she's conceited. She thinks she's pretty."

"She doesn't *think* she's pretty. She *is* pretty. That's two different things."

"Well, let's not argue."

"Who's arguing?"

They watched the game, another of the day's disasters. Dominion School won and Lorinda nearly fainted from frustration. She knew she was better than some of the players and she kept seeing chances to make a pass or score a goal. She was so depressed she could hardly eat her popcorn.

On the way home, Mildred said, "Sarah says you invited her to visit you in Nova Scotia."

"Right."

"I bet it's nice down there in the summertime."

"It is."

"My dad makes a lot of money and he says I can take a train trip next August."

"Lucky you."

"Does the railroad go to Blue Harbour?"

"No."

"But close by?"

"Sixty kilometres. That's far."

"Not so very far." Mildred paused. "I could go. Easy."

"You wouldn't like it."

"Why?"

Lorinda turned and faced her as they reached the corner where they would part. "Because the people down there talk funny. Because some of them call their parents Mummy and Daddy instead of Mom and Dad. Because their winter coats are too long. Because they write good compositions. Because they let girls play on hockey teams."

After Mildred left, Lorinda wondered if she'd blown it again. Mildred was trying to be friendly and she hadn't exactly reached out to meet her half-way.

"Not my day," she sighed, as she opened the front door of 14 Summer Street.

"Lorinda!" called Aunt Marian from the kitchen. "A gentleman came this afternoon to see you and James. He wants to take the two of you to Toronto on Saturday. He says you can each bring a friend. I wouldn't normally let you go somewhere with a stranger, but he is such a distinguished man. I recognized him from his picture in the business section of the *Globe and Mail* last week. And he had a lot of nice things to say about you. His name was Mr. Jackson."

10
A trip to Toronto

Afterwards, Lorinda said that Mr. Jackson's arrival was a real live miracle. "He said he'd come if things got to be awful," she said. "And that's exactly what they were. And that's exactly what he did."

Mr. Jackson arrived at 14 Summer Street at 8:00 A.M. His Peterborough meeting had taken place the day before and he'd stayed at a hotel overnight. He wanted to start early so they could have a good long day in Toronto.

Sarah had already come, but Hank wasn't there yet. Aunt Marian took Mr. Jackson aside. "I hope you're prepared for Hank," she whispered. "You won't believe him till you see him. Holes out of his elbows, grubby boots, and hair that looks like a floor mop — after you've done the floors with it."

"Don't you worry," he said, grinning. Then he looked hard at Aunt Marian. "I was born in the slums myself. Cabbagetown, 1940. I know the ropes."

They all turned around as the doorbell rang.

James rushed to answer it, and there was Hank — scrubbed till he shone, beaming, his hair slicked down on his head. "Hi, Jon," he said.

"Mr. Jackson," corrected Aunt Marian.

"That's all right," he said. "I told Lorinda and James six weeks ago to call me Jon and that goes for their friends too. Now," he said, turning to shake hands with Aunt Marian and Uncle Harry, "we'd better be off. We have a big day ahead of us."

They did so many things that shining, bright February day that it was hard to remember them all afterwards. First, Mr. Jackson took them to a little restaurant in the Yorkville district. Even at 10:30 in the morning it was so dark inside that there were candles on the tables. They each had a hot chocolate before heading off to The World's Biggest Bookstore. They were amazed that there could be so many books all in one place. Mr. Jackson bought them one each. After the long drive to Toronto, he had a good idea what each of them might like. He bought a book on wrestling for Hank; James' book was about animals; to Sarah he gave a book about Israel; and for Lorinda, he found a complete history of hockey.

Then they set off for the CN Tower. They wouldn't forget *that* part of the day. Lorinda looked at the elevator behind its glass window, reaching up five hundred and thirty-three metres, and then she looked at Mr. Jackson. "Jon," she said thoughtfully,

"I don't want to spoil your day, but that thing is almost as high as an airplane."

Jon was, in fact, already looking pale. "Lorinda," he said, "I started working on this airplane phobia thing weeks ago, back home. My therapist suggested that if I got the chance I should try this elevator. He thought it might help to make flying easier for me. I don't have to look out the window until I get to the top. It takes only fifty-eight seconds to get up or down." He laughed shakily. "If I can't handle it, I'll just stay up there permanently."

When the elevator started its ascent, the streets and buildings of Toronto seemed to slide away until Lake Ontario and part of the city were spread out beneath them like a map. It was so beautiful that Lorinda forgot about Mr. Jackson for a few moments. When she looked, his eyes were closed, his fists were clenched and he was trembling. She went over and held his arm. "It's okay," she said. "We're practically there."

And suddenly, they were. Mr. Jackson almost fell out of the elevator while the four kids cheered and congratulated him. Then he looked down at the city from the window.

"It's awful," he gasped, "but at least there's something under us, holding us up. You can't believe what a difference that makes. So once again," he added, his face white but smiling, "you kids have come to my rescue."

On the way down, Mr. Jackson tried to open his eyes a bit, but he couldn't do it for very long. At the bottom, the colour returned to his face and he laughed. "Aren't you ashamed to be seen with such a terrified man?"

"Ashamed!" exclaimed Lorinda. "It's such a relief to find a grown-up who isn't *perfect*."

"Don't feel bad," said Hank. "Even I'm sometimes scared of things."

"Great news!" said Mr. Jackson. "Like what, for instance?"

Hank paused before answering. "Like Aunt Marian," he said.

After they ate lunch in a restaurant (a big place full of wonderful coloured lamps and amazing statues), they went to the Royal Ontario Museum where they saw a real mummy and some reconstructed dinosaurs. At the end of the day, after another meal, Jon drove them back to Peterborough. He whistled to himself as he drove along, and played the radio. There was no one to talk to. All four kids were asleep.

*　　*　　*

The next day was Sunday. Lorinda had no homework to do, so she sat down and worked for an hour with her calligraphy pen. She was getting better every time she practised. She wrote a thank-you letter to Mr. Jackson and even used fancy lettering on the envelope. Finally, she took out the diary that Aunt Joan had given her for Christmas and made an entry for February 12.

Jon took us to Toronto. Hank and Sarah came too. It was wonderful. The buildings were so high and the city was huge, almost like a whole country of buildings. Just before we left, Jon took us to a place where they print things on t-shirts. Everyone got to choose a different colour for their shirt. Mine is red. Jon asked the lady to print our names on the front. Then he said we could have something on the back too. Sarah chose for me, and me for Sarah. Same with Hank and James. It was fun trying to decide. James chose *SUPERMAN* for Hank. Hank asked for *THINKER* on James' shirt. Sarah chose *HOCKEY STAR* for me, and I asked the woman to write *FRIEND* on the back of Sarah's shirt.

We're going to save money from our allowances and buy a shirt (large size) for Mr. Jackson. On the front will be *JON*. It was hard to figure out what to write on the back, but at last we decided. We want the back to say *OUR HERO*.

Lorinda put down her pen, and went in to see James. "Wasn't it great?" she sighed.

"Boy, I'll say," said James.

"It was so great," said Lorinda, "that I don't think I'll even mind if nothing happens on my birthday."

"Hey, wow!" exclaimed James. "It's next Friday. I forgot. But it doesn't matter. I got your present already. It's nice. You'll like it."

"And Mummy and Daddy have sent theirs," remembered Lorinda. "But I don't expect Aunt Marian and Uncle Harry know the date. Even if they do, I can't see Aunt Marian wanting to do anything special for me. And I don't blame her. After all, two days ago I was standing in the front hall yelling awful things at her. And then I went and broke her antique vase. No, I think I'll just skip my birthday this year."

Then she slumped down in the chair by James' bed and sighed. "Four and a half months to go. Oh, brother!"

11
Lorinda's birthday

On the morning of her birthday, Lorinda woke up, stared at the ceiling and thought, I'm eleven, I'm eleven. Then she flopped over onto her stomach and thought some more. I'm almost a teenager. Two more years and I'll be thirteen. She didn't know whether or not she liked that idea, but it was two whole years away, so it didn't really matter. She was bigger than all the girls in her class, but she often felt much younger. It seemed like the only things most of them talked about were boys and clothes. She liked boys a lot (after all, Duncan was her best friend) but she didn't giggle or blush about them the way some of her friends did. And clothes were — well — clothes. She really loved her yellow sweater, but she didn't care one way or another about the rest of her things.

Suddenly James came into her room and yelled, "Happy Birthday!"

"Shhh!" she whispered, putting her finger to her lips. "Don't let them know upstairs. I just couldn't stand it if Aunt Marian felt she had to rush downtown to buy me a present, after all the terrible things I did last Friday. We'll have a little pretend party down here tonight and I'll open your gift and the one from Mummy and Daddy."

School went on as usual. Mildred made a few sour remarks — "If you're eleven, how come you still like doing kid stuff?" and "Just because you're tall doesn't mean you're important" — but this was when people were around to hear. When she was alone with Lorinda she still tried to make friends with her, still hinted about going to Nova Scotia in the summer. Lorinda had almost learned to ignore both sides of Mildred. But often it was hard.

Sarah was as friendly as ever, but she hadn't brought a birthday gift. Lorinda tried not to be disappointed, but she was. Oh, well — maybe with her head cold Sarah hadn't been able to get downtown.

At noon, Aunt Marian still didn't mention Lorinda's birthday. Well, that was fine. Birthdays are for when you're home with your family, surrounded by lots of love. Anyway, maybe Sarah had just forgotten to bring her gift that morning. Maybe she'd bring one in the afternoon.

But she didn't. Mr. O'Reilly wished Lorinda a happy birthday right in front of the whole class, which was nice, but it wasn't like being in Blue Harbour with Duncan and Fiona and George and

Glynis all singing "Happy Birthday" at the top of their lungs on the Government Wharf. That had happened last year. The lobster fishermen had looked up from their boats and joined in the song.

I'd better not start thinking like *that*, thought Lorinda, or first thing you know, I'll be howling all over my English composition. She threw herself into the story she was writing and almost forgot her troubles. Writing always did that for her. It was like letting a bunch of bees out of a box. The bees were still alive, but the awful buzzing stopped.

There was another hockey game after school. Lorinda always went to the games so people wouldn't think she was a poor sport, but she hated them. She sat chomping her popcorn extra hard, because it made her so mad to see the team missing all those goals. She was dying, just *dying*, to be out there. Duke of York lost again, this time to St. Anthony's.

It was late when she and James got home, and already dark. Dinner would be late that night because of the hockey game. Even after a whole tub of popcorn, Lorinda was starved.

"One thing about Aunt Marian," she said as they turned up the path to the front door, "she can really cook."

They opened the door and let themselves in, stamped the snow off their feet, put their boots in the corner and hung up their coats in the porch closet. Then James yelled, "We're home!"

Aunt Marian and Uncle Harry came out to the front hall. Aunt Marian was wearing her best dress and had obviously just come from the hairdresser.

"Wow!" exclaimed Lorinda. She couldn't help it. "Do you ever look pretty!"

"Happy Birthday," said Uncle Harry. Aunt Marian came forward and very carefully, very stiffly, kissed Lorinda on the cheek.

"Come on in," she said.

And there in the living room, winking and sparkling from every table and from the mantelpiece and the big rolltop desk, were dozens of flickering candles. A fire crackled in the fireplace. In the dining room behind, Lorinda could see streamers and balloons decorating the walls.

"Oh, Aunt Marian!" she gasped, sitting down hard on the nearest chair. "I didn't think I cared about this birthday, but I guess I really did." She jumped up and rushed over to her Aunt, almost knocking her over with a bear hug. "Thank you!" she cried. Then she hugged Uncle Harry, who said, "There, there, Lorinda!" James just beamed.

While Lorinda was looking at the pile of gifts on the floor under the oval table, the doorbell rang. When she turned around to see who it was, there were Hank and Sarah holding packages and grinning.

"I thought I'd burst all day," laughed Sarah, "trying to pretend I didn't even have a gift for you."

"Here!" said Hank gruffly, shoving his gift into her hands.

Aunt Marian came in carrying a tray of long-stemmed glasses filled with pop and orange juice. Even Hank, with his not-very-clean face, handled his fancy glass with as much skill as a headwaiter.

"After all," James was to say later, "a wrestler's got beautiful co-ordination. He couldn't have spilled that drink if he'd tried."

While they snacked on peanuts and corn chips, Lorinda opened her gifts: a package of construction paper and crayons from Jessie; a little camera and some film from her parents; a photo album from James, who knew all about the camera; a tin of caramel corn from Hank; a little gold chain from Sarah; an envelope with money in it from Uncle Harry for buying more films.

The last present was from Aunt Marian. As Lorinda pulled the gift from its tissue-paper nest, she gasped. It was a blouse — pale blue with a drawstring neckline embroidered with flowers. Whatever had made her think she didn't care about clothes? She hugged the blouse to her, eyes shining. "Oh, Aunt Marian! I love it! Where did you buy it?"

Aunt Marian looked shy but pleased. "I didn't buy it anywhere," she said. "I made it."

There was a little silence. Lorinda stared at her aunt. "You *made* it?"

"Yes."

"For *me?* Specially?" Maybe she had made it for someone else who had moved away or died or something.

"For you," said Aunt Marian. "Specially."

"Just a sec. Hang on for a few minutes, you guys," said Lorinda and dashed off to the basement. Quickly she changed into her best jeans, brushed her hair and put on the blouse. She grinned at herself in the mirror. She came very close to looking pretty.

When she went upstairs, Uncle Harry clapped his hands and cried, "Pretty! A very pretty girl!"

"Anyone could look pretty in this blouse," grinned Lorinda. "Thank you, Aunt Marian."

Then they had dinner — Lorinda's favourite things: fried chicken and frozen corn on the cob, with hot fudge sundaes and birthday cake for dessert. When they were back in the living room, Lorinda said to her aunt and uncle, "You couldn't have done another single thing to make it a nicer day."

"Don't be so sure," said James, looking like he was going to burst.

Uncle Harry went upstairs to the back hall and brought down what looked like a large box with a big blanket over it. "Presto!" he cried, removing the blanket.

Lorinda couldn't say anything for two long minutes. She just stared. First at the gift, then at Uncle Harry, and especially at Aunt Marian — who was looking nervous but different. How, different? She was looking *happy*.

Finally Lorinda could speak.

"A cat!" she breathed. "A real live cat!" She went carefully to the cage and squatted down to open the door. A very sleepy cat came out slowly, yawned, stretched, then rubbed his warm head against Lorinda's knee. Large, grey, and purring loudly, the cat moved from person to person, rubbing legs, yawning some more, stretching.

"It was Marian's idea," said Uncle Harry.

Lorinda picked up the cat. He was heavy and soft and warm and alive. She turned to Aunt Marian. "If you live to be a hundred and twenty-three years old, you'll never be able to get anyone a nicer present. Ever."

Aunt Marian was sitting very still and straight, but her eyes were bright and she was smiling.

"I couldn't find a cow small enough," she said with a little laugh. "But I wanted the biggest small animal we could find. They told us at the Humane

Society that he was gentle and friendly and kind of sleepy."

"We were afraid he'd meow and spoil the surprise," said Uncle Harry, grinning. "But we needn't have worried. He slept through the whole party." Everybody laughed.

"The cage is yours too," said James, hugging himself. "To use when we take him home with us in July."

Lorinda shut her eyes and sighed. She not only had him, she had him for keeps. "I'm calling him Gretzky," she said, burying her face in his fur. "I love him so much I could faint." When she looked up, there were tears in her eyes.

After everyone had gone home, James and Uncle Harry washed the dishes. Lorinda and Aunt Marian sat down beside the fire in the living room. Gretzky was asleep again on Lorinda's lap.

"How could you give me such a wonderful party," asked Lorinda, stroking Gretzky, "after I yelled all those awful things at you? And after I broke your vase?"

Aunt Marian was actually looking relaxed. Without the line between her eyebrows, she was a very pretty woman.

"Because pretty nearly everything you said was true," she answered. "After I got over being hurt and angry, I thought about everything you shouted at me. After a day or two, I realized that I *needed* to hear those things. And when I saw you with Mr. Jackson, a man you didn't even know very well, I thought some more. I tried to figure out why you were happy with him and miserable with me."

"And?"

"I decided it was because everyone was giving and relaxing and loving instead of instructing and correcting and worrying."

"Oh."

"I can't promise miracles, Lorinda. But I can try to loosen up a little. Poor old Uncle Harry might like that better too."

Lorinda remembered Uncle Harry's "There, there, Marian."

"But the vase, though," she said.

This time, Aunt Marian laughed right out loud. "Lorinda," she said, "my own great-aunt Susie gave me that vase when I was ten. For my tenth birthday. I'd been hoping for a doll. I always hated it, but she was a stern old lady and I felt I had to keep it around. Even after she died, it got to be a habit to have it on a table somewhere. Every time we moved, I hauled it out and put it on display. At least in this house I got it as far away as the basement."

"So it wasn't so terrible, after all?"

"No, Lorinda, it wasn't. At the time, I think I wanted you to feel guilty because I was still hurt and angry. But you really did me a favour. That vase never looked so pretty to me as when it was in a hundred pieces."

"Aunt Marian," exclaimed Lorinda, "we're really talking!"

"That's right. And maybe we'll get better and better at it. It's hard to know how to speak to children if you've never had any." Aunt Marian sighed. "Lorinda . . ."

"Yes?"

"I always wanted a little girl."

"Oh."

Then Aunt Marian frowned for a moment, as though trying to decide whether or not to say something. "I had a baby once," she said finally.

"You!" Lorinda gasped and the cat nearly fell out of her lap. "What happened? Oh, Aunt Marian!"

"It was retarded. But I loved it. It died."

Lorinda put the cat on the floor and went over to sit closer to Aunt Marian. "What was it?" she asked her.

"A boy. But I wanted both. A girl and a boy. Maybe more."

"And?"

"That was all. I never had any more babies. Sometimes that happens. You want them, but they just don't come. After a while it made me too sad to even think about children. And I guess I kind of froze up inside and forgot how to be soft and warm with people." She sighed again. "Poor Uncle Harry." Then she looked at Lorinda. "Maybe you can help me learn how."

Lorinda laughed and gave her aunt's hand a squeeze. "You don't have to take lessons from me, Aunt Marian. You're a real quick learner. You seem to know exactly what to do already."

Aunt Marian rose from the chair as Uncle Harry and James came back from the kitchen. "Time for bed, you two," she announced. She turned to Lorinda and smiled. "Don't think I'm going to stop ordering you around. That's half the fun of being a parent."

"Hey, Aunt Marian," said Lorinda at the head of the stairs, "what will you do with Gretzky when we're at school? He may scratch the furniture, you know."

"I know," said Aunt Marian. "It was one of the first things I thought of. Well, if he does, he does. But he looks too lazy and slow to do much scratching. I guess learning about cats is another thing I'll have to do while I'm learning about children. Besides" — she grinned and looked at James — "James has already told me I need a cow."

Lorinda and James turned and hugged their aunt and uncle goodnight. Aunt Marian hugged them back, as though she really meant it. That's because she did.

12
The thief

A week from the following Monday, something else disappeared from the school — a little silver electric clock from the library. The president of the Home and School Association had donated it the year before. It was discovered to be missing at noon. Lorinda had been in the library in the morning.

"Oh-ho!" said Mildred to Lorinda.

"What do you mean, oh-ho?" snapped Lorinda.

"You know exactly what I mean."

"Yes, I think I do. But how about saying it right out?"

"Well," said Mildred, with a small tight smile, "what were you doing in the library this morning between classes?"

"Looking up brontosaurus in the encyclopedia."

"Many people in there?"

"No."

"Hmmmm!"

Lorinda sat down at her desk with her chest tight. My gosh, she thought, this year is really something. Every time I think that I might even *like* living in this town, something awful happens.

She sighed and turned to Sarah. "I hope they have a hockey team at the jail they put me in."

Sarah didn't laugh. "Don't joke about things like that," she said. "Someone told me they're going to bring in the police after school this afternoon. They're going to question people who are known to have been in the rooms where things were missing. I just thought I should tell you so it wouldn't come as a surprise."

A tight knot of fear formed in the centre of Lorinda's chest. She couldn't keep her mind on her work, even during English period, which she usually loved. Once, when Mr. O'Reilly asked her a question, she didn't even answer and he had to speak to her twice.

Mildred poked her in the ribs. "What's the matter?" she whispered. "Your conscience bothering you?"

"No!" exclaimed Lorinda. "But yours should be bothering *you*."

"Why? I haven't done anything. I haven't stolen anything."

Lorinda felt like getting up from her desk and running as fast as she could down the hall, out of the school and all the way back to Nova Scotia. But she just sat like a stone and said nothing. Mr.

O'Reilly looked at her oddly. "Anything wrong, Lorinda? You look pale."

"No," she said. "I'm fine." Just dandy, she thought, just dandy.

On the way home for lunch, she told James how she felt. "I'm so used to Mildred acting like I'm guilty that I almost feel guilty. I bet I even *look* guilty. Even Mr. O'Reilly asked me this morning if anything was wrong."

A soft, wet, depressing snow was falling. Lorinda picked some up and made a snowball, throwing it absently at a tree.

"Gee," said James, "this sure is a tough year for you. I thought after your wonderful birthday party that all your troubles were over. But I guess not."

"I guess not too," she sighed.

* * *

In the middle of the afternoon, Lorinda had a brain wave. She was sitting in the classroom in silent reading period, idly watching the handyman as he checked the bulbs in the hall. That guy must be so sick of checking and rechecking those things day after day — ever since I came, she thought. She looked at his long, skinny body and his frowning face. No wonder he's frowning. He's bored right out of his skull.

Ever since I came. The words repeated themselves in her mind. He's everywhere, she thought. He has to check everything — the classrooms, the washrooms, the library, the general purpose room. *There's no place he doesn't go.*

The more she thought about it, the more sure Lorinda was that the handyman had something to do with the thefts in the school. But she had no idea what to do about it. She couldn't tell the teacher. That would be tattling, especially as she didn't have any proof. She couldn't just walk up to the handyman and tell him she thought he was a thief. What if he wasn't? She knew only too well what it was like to be accused of something you hadn't done. What else could she do?

Suddenly she knew. She could catch him in the act.

When the bell rang for recess, the handyman was still changing bulbs right outside the classroom. To James, who had come upstairs to meet her, Lorinda said in a loud voice, "It's wet out. I'm going to leave my watch on my desk. It's expensive, and I don't want to ruin it in the snow."

When they had turned the corner, she told James her plan. They would stay behind after everyone had gone out for recess and see what happened. If Lorinda was wrong about the handyman, they would look very suspicious inside the school with their coats on, but they had to take that chance.

James stationed himself by the outer door downstairs and Lorinda hid in the staff washroom across the hall. Before long, there was the scrape of a ladder as the handyman climbed down. Then she heard him cross the hall. Through a chink in the washroom door, she watched him enter her classroom. Slowly, silently, she pushed the door all the way open and followed him. Peeking into the room, she saw him cross over to her desk, snatch up her watch and stuff it into the back pocket of his overalls. Lorinda raced back to the washroom, her heart beating wildly.

When she came out, he was back on the ladder. She went over to where he was and looked up. "I saw you," she said. "I saw you take my watch."

The man looked like a cornered animal. He hunched his shoulders, and his eyes widened with fear. For one moment he was perfectly still. Then he leapt off the ladder and raced for the outer door. There was no way anything but a guided missile could have caught him before he reached the stairs.

But James was downstairs, waiting. As the man flew out the door, James tore after him. Then, in a flying leap, he shot through the air and tackled the man's legs. Down they both came into the soft snow. Immediately, a crowd formed around them.

Lorinda arrived, panting, and broke into the group. "I saw him!" she cried. "I saw him take my watch!"

The man was on his feet now, calm again. "Little liar!" he growled. "Who does she think she is?"

Lorinda pointed. "Look in his back pocket," she said. The man tried to run again, but suddenly Mr. O'Reilly was there, holding him gently, firmly. One of the grade eight boys reached over and took the watch from the handyman's pocket.

The handyman slumped down in the snow and put his head in his hands.

Lorinda suddenly felt sick. She was relieved that finally everyone would know she wasn't the thief, but she didn't like the look of that poor man drooped over in the wet snow. She wasn't going to jail, but maybe someone else was — all because of her. Her thoughts whirled. She knew you couldn't just let people steal things. And she knew how easy it was to suspect the wrong person. Still, she didn't like it, she didn't like looking at that man in the snow. When the police came to take him away, she went somewhere else so she wouldn't have to watch.

Around the corner of the building, she found James, crying. "I know exactly how you feel," she said, putting an arm around his shoulders. "You did a real good job, and I guess it had to be done. But I sure wish there'd been another way to find out I wasn't the thief. It's all my fault."

"It's okay, Lorinda," said James, sniffing loudly and blowing his nose. "It was kind of fun for a few minutes there. I *enjoyed* the tackle. I felt like a hero. But then" — he sighed and blew his nose again — "when I saw him scrunched down there in the slush like a scared rabbit in a trap — well, it was so . . ." He paused.

"I know," said Lorinda. "I agree. It was."

After school, James and Lorinda walked home in silence. When they arrived, they told Aunt Marian the whole tale. Then they took turns holding Gretzky. It was comforting to feel his big furry body and hear his motorboat purr. "Every bit as good as a cow," said James to Lorinda.

*　　*　　*

By the next day, it seemed that everyone knew all about what had happened. In the thief's apartment the police found bracelets, rings, pocket knives, wallets. Some of the missing things weren't there because they'd been sold, but they found Mildred's pen and Mr. O'Reilly's camera and the little silver clock from the library.

"How did you get the idea that it might be the handyman?" asked Mr. O'Reilly during first period.

"Oh, I dunno," said Lorinda. "Probably because

he came when I did, and I knew the robberies started almost the minute I set foot in the school. He was trying to fix our projector the very first day I arrived, the day Mildred's pen disappeared, when he kept turning the lights on and off. I was afraid someone might think it was me."

Everyone laughed. Mildred laughed harder than anyone. Lorinda was careful not to look at her.

"Don't you worry about that, Lorinda," grinned Wayne Gretzky. "No one would ever think a thing like that."

"Teacher's pet!" muttered Mildred behind her atlas.

13
The big game

The next morning, James and Lorinda found two letters addressed to them in the mailbox. One was a joint letter from their father and mother.

Dear Lorinda and James,

Thank you for your wonderful letters. We're so lonesome for you both, it makes us feel a lot better every time we hear from you.

Here in Texas, we're fine. Jessie loves the animals. She goes out every day to see the baby pigs. She misses you, and sometimes when there's a knock on the door, she cries out, "Lorinda? James?" and rushes to open it, so you don't need to worry about her forgetting you.

Daddy is getting much better. He coughs less often, and he has started to go out to the barn to help Uncle John with the animals. He has a good tan and looks very handsome.

Say hi to Aunt Marian and Uncle Harry. Also, give my love to Sarah and Hank. Even though I've never met them, I feel they are my special friends. I hope they can each come to visit us in Nova Scotia.

Your dad is going to finish off the page.

Love,
Mummy

Hi, kids,

How are things? Have they caught the thief yet? Tell Hank that when he comes to Blue Harbour I want to learn how to wrestle. Tell Sarah that we'll take her clam digging when she visits. Tell Aunt Marian and Uncle Harry that they have to come and see us too. Tell yourselves that I love you a lot.

Love,
Daddy

P.S. And I miss you like a son-of-a-gun.

The next letter was shorter. It was from Duncan.

Dear Lorinda,

I'm on the school hockey team this year. I hope this doesn't make you feel bad. That Peterborough coach must be crazy or blind or something. Doesn't he want to win any games?

Fiona and me miss you and James. Fiona

says to tell James to write and say if he has anything growing in his planter. Your calligraphy writing is real good. I'll have to go away for six months so someone can give me one for a present too. Ha-ha.

Your friend,
Duncan

After reading the letters, Lorinda left for school early. Sarah wanted to try out for the school play that morning and Lorinda had promised to go with her. After she'd gone, Aunt Marian spoke to James at the front door.

"I'm sorry there was no special letter for you, James," she said.

"That's okay, Aunt Marian." He sighed. "Glynis, my best friend in Blue Harbour, can't write yet, so she sends all her messages in George's letters to Lorinda. I know she'd write if she could. Besides," he added, "don't forget last week she sent me that neat picture she drew of Petunia."

Aunt Marian smiled. "I'm going to really miss you when you leave. Both of you." Then she gave James a questioning look. "Does a boy who's almost eight think he's too old for a goodbye hug?"

James laughed. "Holy crumb, no!" he said. "My dad says that if it's a crime for a boy to be hugged after the age of ten, then he's been a criminal for thirty years. We're big on hugs in our family."

So Aunt Marian gave James a big hug and he left for school, kicking ice balls along the sidewalk, whistling. The weather was cold again and the snow squeaked beneath his boots as he walked along.

*   *   *

This was the day of the last hockey game before the playoffs. If Duke of York didn't win against Ashburnham, they wouldn't be able to play anymore this season. Everyone was excited and nervous, even Lorinda. The class couldn't keep their minds on history and geography that afternoon, so Mr. O'Reilly finally settled for a spelling bee. He chose Mildred and Lorinda as team captains. Mildred's team won. She was all sugary sweetness to Lorinda for the rest of the afternoon. Lorinda laughed and said to Sarah, "I suppose if a train ran over me and cut my head right off, she'd think I was just about perfect."

Around 3:30, everyone spilled out of the school and headed up Sherbrooke Street to the rink. Inside, they all kept their heavy winter coats on against the sharp, damp chill. Their breath hung in the air like little puffs of cold smoke. There was a lot of shouting back and forth between the spectators and the teams. The air was sizzling with excitement.

The Duke of York coach was striding up and down, looking frantic.

"Horace Doherty and John Kalami haven't turned up," someone yelled. "They have the flu. If Jerry Stevenson doesn't come, the team won't have enough players."

But Jerry arrived and Mr. Zomer started to look calmer. Before long, the whistle blew and there was a moment of complete silence as they all focused on the face-off.

Duke of York had been improving all month, but with Horace Doherty off the team, they were in trouble. Horace was their best forward, and an aggressive player. The Duke of York cheering section tried to make up for his absence by screaming as loudly as they could.

Jerry Stevenson was a fast skater and a good shot, but he couldn't seem to get near the net. Whenever he passed the puck, the receiver missed it. Ashburnham got the first goal and the rink exploded with cheers.

Soon after, Jerry scored and the Duke of York students rocked the stands, jumping up and down and shrieking. Then another goal for Ashburnham. And another.

The game was already into the third period. The spectators tensed as Jerry Stevenson flew down the ice with the puck. He stopped. He poised his stick to shoot. It looked like a sure thing. Then it happened. One of the Ashburnham players tripped right into Jerry's path. Jerry fell over the player. His stick flew from his hand and he landed hard on the ice, his foot bent under him. He couldn't even get up. The team manager and the coach had to come on the ice to help him hobble off.

There was time-out for ten minutes to find out if Jerry could continue playing. Finally, the announcement came over the loudspeaker. There was a doctor at the rink — one of the fathers — and he said that although Jerry's foot wasn't broken, it was sprained and he would have to keep off the ice for at least three weeks. The Duke of York cheering section slumped down in the stands, faces glum.

Mr. Zomer emerged from the dressing room and stared grimly at the empty ice. It is hard to see two months of hard work go up in smoke. Suddenly he stiffened and scanned the bleachers. Rapidly his eyes darted over the group from Duke of York. Then he found what he was looking for.

"Lorinda!" he shouted.

She stood up.

"Get down here — fast!"

She raced down to join him on the ice.

"Will you?" he said.

"Will I what?"

"Play."

Her heart sank. "I don't have my skates with me," she groaned.

"C'mon!" He took her by the arm and hauled her off to the dressing room.

"Hand me out Jerry's skates," he yelled. "And his socks. And his uniform. There," he said, passing them to Lorinda. "Now get in the girls' washroom and make those skates fit!"

"Oh, please, please, please!" murmured Lorinda as she pushed her feet into the skates.

They fit! When she first put them on, they were a bit loose, but with Jerry's hockey socks over her own thick woolly ones from home, it felt almost as if the skates had been bought especially for her. She struggled out of her clothes and into Jerry's pants and top. She took an elastic out of her pocket and tied her hair in a knot at the back of her head. Then she put on the helmet and fastened it. She was ready.

"Hey, Aunt Marian," she said to the empty washroom, "here go my front teeth!"

She wasn't even nervous. Excited, yes, but not nervous in that awful way when your mouth dries out and your knees shake. She loved this game and everything about it — the feel of the ice disappearing behind her flying skates, the smell of the dressing room, of the wool socks, of the ice itself, a clear fresh smell that was a mixture of steel and frozen water and popcorn and people.

She shot onto the ice like a bullet and took up her position. She was glad now that she'd come to every game and gone to those weekly practices. She was familiar with every player, and she'd been a part of every manoeuvre. The team knew what to expect from her too.

Down in the dressing room, she had thought about the score and the time remaining. At 3-1 for Ashburnham, they needed three more goals to win the game — and they had only ten minutes to score them.

Two minutes after the face-off, Lorinda blasted the puck to David Jones, who was staked out in a good position near the goal. He caught it. He shot. He *scored*. The Duke of York fans yelled and pounded their feet on the floorboards.

Then Lorinda really came into her own. She fired a shot from centre ice with a power strong enough to send it flying off an intercepting stick, right into the net. The crowd screamed, "Lorinda! Lorinda!"

Now Lorinda was racing up and down the rink, her feet like wings. Passing, intercepting, searching for a pathway for a clear shot. She could feel the end of the game getting closer and closer. Then, at last, another chance. She swooped near the net as David

Jones sent the puck skidding across the ice to her. With all her might, she shot it through the goalie's feet, straight into the net. It was so fast, he didn't even see it coming.

Moments later, after the face-off, the whistle blew. The game was over and Duke of York had won! The uproar from the stands was deafening.

After all the excitement and congratulations, the coach spoke to Lorinda as she came out from the girls' washroom. "Some hockey player!" he said, beaming.

Then he stopped smiling for a moment. "I apologize, Lorinda. I made you unhappy, and all for nothing. I'll admit something to you. I wasn't really worried about you getting hurt. I could see from the practices that you knew how to look after yourself as well as any of the boys. I just didn't think a girl would be able to stand up to the tensions of competitive hockey. I never had any sisters and my own children are boys. I don't really know much about girls. I knew you were good, but I figured you might conk out on us when we needed you most." He laughed and shook her hand. "Instead, you *rescued* us. Thank you, and welcome to the team!"

By the time Lorinda went out into the arena, most of the kids had gone home. But James and Hank and Sarah were there waiting for her. And someone else — Aunt Marian.

"I was just passing by," she said, "and I thought I'd come in and watch for a while. Parents are supposed to be interested in their children's activities." She laughed. "And Lorinda, I was there when that boy hurt his foot, so I saw you come out on the ice and save the game. I was so proud! And listen, I understand now. About the teeth, I mean. If I could skate like that — if I could whizz up and down the ice and weave in and out and then send that puck sailing into the net the way you did — I don't think I'd be one speck worried about *my* teeth, either. Come along, now. It's late. I was too excited to leave. I think our whole family will have Kentucky Fried Chicken for supper."

Our whole family! That's how Aunt Marian thinks of us now, thought Lorinda. James looked at his aunt. Not many people have two families, he thought. Like us.

14
A family of five

February passed, and March. They were a family of five, now, with Gretzky playing a special part. When Lorinda and James were at school, he slept on a cushion on the green velvet chair in the living room, or snoozed in the kitchen while Aunt Marian cooked. When Uncle Harry sat in his chair in front of the TV, Gretzky often curled up in his lap. His purr was so loud, it was like a song.

At school, Mr. O'Reilly shunted the seats around. Mildred ended up on the other side of the room, with someone other than Lorinda to torment.

"What's wrong with that kid?" exclaimed Lorinda to James. "She's not happy unless she's making somebody miserable."

"I dunno," said James. "I guess someone must be tormenting *her* somewhere. Maybe at home, where she can't fight back. Hank says there's a family in his neighbourhood like that. One boy is real mean to his little sister all the time because his big brother is mean to him. Kinda tough on the little sister."

In the meantime, James was growing so many plants in his planter, and they were getting so big that Uncle Harry had to go downtown and buy him a bunch of new pots. "His room looks like an experimental farm," he chuckled.

Although Lorinda and Sarah had other friends, they spent most of their free time together making plans, sharing secrets, roaring with laughter over crazy jokes. Lorinda loved Sarah's house, with its strange abstract paintings on the walls, the often unfamiliar, but delicious food, Sarah's warm, kind mother. At 14 Summer Street, Aunt Marian discovered that Sarah loved chocolate marshmallow cookies and made sure she always had a tin of them around. James spent half his life at Hank's house, enjoying the family of seven noisy kids.

March rolled on towards April and the hockey season began to wind down. Aunt Marian attended nearly every game, and Uncle Harry came when he could. Duke of York didn't win the trophy, but they came pretty close, hanging on till the last game, when Dominion scored the winning goal in the last second of play. Lorinda's team nearly collapsed with disappointment, but they found they could still eat the heaps of hot dogs and potato chips the coach served at a party following the game. They'd been a good team and they knew it.

"Hey, Lorinda," cried Jerry, whose foot had mended, "you'll have to come up here from Nova Scotia next year and help us out in the play-offs!"

"The play-offs!" scoffed Horace Doherty. "We wouldn't even have *gotten* to the play-offs without Lorinda."

"I wish you could play with us again too, Lorinda," said the coach.

"So do I," sighed Lorinda. She knew that leaving Peterborough was going to be almost as hard as arriving.

At last it was April. Little by little the last puddles of snow melted. Then, with a thundering swiftness, summer arrived. One day they were in winter jackets, the next they were toasting their bare arms in the sun.

"No spring," said Lorinda to James as she lay in the hammock on the third of May. "They don't have any spring here. You just go slam bang from winter into summer."

"Pretty weird," agreed James. "But nice too."

By June 15, there'd been a week-long heat wave and they weren't so sure how nice it was. They weren't used to the humid heat and they wilted like cooked flowers. Aunt Marian went downtown and bought them extra cool clothes to help them survive until the weather broke. Gretzky lay around in shady places, pretending he wasn't wearing a fur coat.

On June 18, a letter came from Blue Harbour. It was from Mr. Dauphinee. Lorinda read it aloud to the family at supper.

Dear Kids,

We're home! I'm as fit as a fiddle and haven't had a cough for two months. The doctor says he can't believe I'm me. But I am.

If Jessie could count, she'd be counting the days till you come home. Her favourite question is "When?" We answer, "Soon!"

We'll be waiting for you and Gretzky at the airport on the afternoon of July 3. I wish we had a brass band to greet you as you come off the plane. There ought to be music playing to tell you how happy we'll be to see you again.

Love to Aunt Marian and Uncle Harry.

Love,
Daddy

Two more weeks! Lorinda held the letter in her lap and stared into space. In two more weeks, they'd be home. "Oh, James," she breathed. "I can hardly believe it's so soon."

But James was looking at Aunt Marian and

Uncle Harry. They were smiling because that's what they felt they should be doing, but the sadness in their eyes was terrible to see.

"Why can't you come down and live with us in Blue Harbour?" he sighed. "You and Hank and Sarah and the CN Tower and the Kawartha Lakes and the Lift-Lock and the zoo?"

Lorinda looked at them too, and her heart was confused and troubled. "I guess we want everything," she said. "I know *I* do. I want you two to come with us, and the whole hockey team, and Mr. O'Reilly's English classes. And Sarah." She laughed suddenly. "But I think I'll survive without Mildred."

"You may not have to," grinned Aunt Marian. "In the grocery store yesterday, I heard her mother telling Mrs. Johnson that Mildred was going to visit a friend in Nova Scotia this summer."

Lorinda put both hands over her eyes. Then she laughed. "Oh, well," she said, "after being stuffed into our tiny little house for a few days, with rain outside and the foghorn keeping her awake at night and salt mackerel for lunch, I don't think she'd stay long."

"Or . . ." said James. "Well . . . who knows?"

"Right," agreed Lorinda. "Who knows."

*   *   *

On July 2, the day before they were to leave, James

and Lorinda got a card in the mail from Mr. Jackson.

Hi Guys,

 Have fun on the plane. Eat slowly, because you won't have an extra dinner this time. If I ever get brave enough to fly again (I took the train home), I promise you one thing: I'll send you two free tickets so you can come along too.

Love and thanks,
Jon Jackson

The day Lorinda and James left Peterborough was a sad one. Sarah and Hank came to see them before they set off for the airport. Sarah was crying so hard she couldn't speak. She just handed Lorinda a small package and hugged her hard.

 "Write!" said Lorinda. "Write lots of letters. And come see us soon. You're the best girlfriend I ever had."

 Sarah could only moan.

 Hank wasn't crying, but his eyes were red. His hair was as wild as ever and his face was dirty. "I never had no friend like you before, James," he said.

 "Me neither," said James. "And I guess I never will."

 Hank handed him a box. "Don't open it till you're on the airplane," he said. "It's special."

Lorinda opened Sarah's gift. It was a gold chain bracelet to match her necklace. "Let's go," she said in a choked voice. "If we don't get out of here soon, I'm gonna cry so hard we'll have to swim to Nova Scotia."

She and James piled into the car, where Aunt Marian and Uncle Harry were waiting. Gretzky was already asleep in his cage on the back seat.

*   *   *

At the airport, the goodbyes were awful. Everybody hugged everybody else, and Aunt Marian said, "Thank you for making us into a family for six months. You changed my whole life." There were tears in her eyes.

Uncle Harry said, "There, there, Marian." Then he added, embarrassed, "My life too."

Aunt Marian cleared her throat. "Guess what!" she said.

"What?" said James.

"What?" said Lorinda.

"We're going to try to adopt a baby."

"Aunt Marian!" cried Lorinda. "Wow!"

"But we're a little bit old," Aunt Marian went on, "so it may take a while. They like to give the babies to younger couples. So . . ."

"So?"

This time it was Uncle Harry's turn to speak.

"So on the way home," he said, "I'm going to take Aunt Marian to the Humane Society so we can pick out a cat to keep us company in the meantime." Suddenly he chuckled. "It's not just you two we're going to miss, you know. After all, there are *three* of you leaving!"

"Oh, Uncle Harry!" beamed Lorinda.

"Hurry!" yelled the flight attendant from the doorway.

So they ran to catch the plane.

* * *

Inside the plane, Lorinda and James fastened their seatbelts. Then James put Hank's box on his lap. It was wrapped in brown paper.

"Open it!" cried Lorinda. "I can hardly wait."

Slowly James took the paper off the parcel. Then he opened the box. "Oh, Lorinda!" She could hardly hear his voice.

"What? What is it?"

James hugged the box close to his chest.

"Well, *say* something, for Pete's sake! What's the matter? What *is* it?"

"It's his wrestling trophy," said James. "From the competition in March. The only one he ever won."

He turned and stared out the window. One large tear rolled down his cheek.

A stewardess stopped at their seat. "What's the matter with the little boy?" she asked Lorinda. "Is he sick? Or is he afraid of the plane?"

"No," said Lorinda. "He's just had a beautiful, terrible shock. He'll be fine."

15
Home again

The reunion at the airport was perfect. Jessie ran up and down the terminal corridor shrieking with joy, her black curls jiggling like crazy. She kept hugging James and Lorinda over and over again. Lorinda had forgotten how good her warm, sturdy little body felt. Mr. Dauphinee was looking strong and healthy and tall and handsome. Mrs. Dauphinee looked like — well, their mother. Lorinda suddenly felt complete. How could she describe it? She'd often been happy in the past six months, but she'd felt like a circle with a gap in the circumference. Now the circle was closed, round, perfect.

In the car on their way to Blue Harbour, the air exploded with everyone's news, everyone's adventures. However, as they turned off the main highway onto the shore road, James and Lorinda fell silent.

In front of them, the whitecaps were racing out of the Bay, the surf breaking high and white on the islands. The houses and buildings were all familiar now. They passed their favourite fish stores and the red lobster factory and the little bakery. There were the beaches with the waves crashing on the shore and, in between, the rocks — large and solid and full of memories. A boat with crowds of seagulls wheeling low above it headed for one of the smaller coves. Through the open window, they could hear the bellbuoy and the Groaner.

"This is my place," said James softly.

"Oh, James," said Lorinda, "I was trying to think of the right way to say it, and you just went and did it. You're right. It's our place. This is where we belong."

Then they rounded the corner and Blue Harbour spread out beneath them. As they drove down the hill into the U-shaped cove, they passed Mac-Dermid's Gift Shoppe, Coolen's Variety Store, the gas station, the Himmelmans' house, Mr. Hyson's hill.

"I feel as though I've been running for months and months," said Lorinda, "and now I can sit down and rest."

Then their house was in front of them, broken porch and all. Petunia was munching grass on the front lawn, and the geraniums were in bloom in the window boxes.

As their car turned into the driveway, there was a loud cheer and four heads popped up from behind the fence: Duncan, Fiona, George and Glynis. "Welcome home!" they yelled.

"That circle is getting rounder and rounder every minute," cried Lorinda as she and James both dashed out of the car to greet their friends.

Back in the car, Mrs. Dauphinee opened Gretzky's cage. Sleepily, he yawned and stretched, then jumped out onto the front lawn. Moving over to a huge bark pot full of nasturtiums, he leapt up and sat in the middle of them. Then he lay down and fell asleep.

Mr. and Mrs. Dauphinee laughed.

"Well!" said Mr. Dauphinee. "There goes *that* part of my garden."

Mrs. Dauphinee went over to stroke Gretzky's soft head. "I guess he knows where he belongs too," she said.